SEARCHING
FOR
THE TRUTH

BARBARA BIRCHIM

authorHOUSE

AuthorHouse™
1663 Liberty Drive
Bloomington, IN 47403
www.authorhouse.com
Phone: 833-262-8899

Published by AuthorHouse 03/11/2021

ISBN: 978-1-6655-1947-2 (sc)
ISBN: 978-1-6655-1961-8 (e)

Library of Congress Control Number: 2021905036

Print information available on the last page.

Cover Design - Leslie Clark, Larkspur Studio
Editor – Sue J. Clark Literary Specialties

ACKNOWLEDGMENTS

To my Vietnam helicopter pilot guru who has done hours of research on my case, I couldn't have gotten as far in my quest for answers without you. Your endless interviews with others who led to more information and leads has been amazing. Bob, I cannot thank you enough times for your continued support to find the last piece to this puzzle.

To Jerry, my husband's last state-side commander, thank you for continuing to support me in my search to get answers and for reading the manuscript and giving me suggestions to clarify certain points.

To my friend Marilyn who read the manuscript and gave their thoughts, a big thank you.

Also by Barbara Birchim

Is Anybody Listening? A True Story About
The POW/MIAs In The Vietnam War

The Adventures of Charles Dunkin A Very Special Bear

DEDICATION

This book is dedicated to my family and all the families that continue to wait for their missing loved ones to come home.

LET ME INTRODUCE MYSELF

My name is Barbara Birchim and as a result of my husband being listed as Missing In Action during the Vietnam War, I have become a pseudo detective. Over the past 53 years, I've learned that networking with various military and veteran organizations, along with searching in archives was paramount to finding answers to the questions in my first book, Is Anybody Listening? A True Story About The POW/MIAs In The Vietnam War. That book is non-fiction and addresses, by name, the men and places in my husband's story. I also share with the reader what happens to me as I made the long journey to find the complicated answers.

Searching For The Truth, is fiction based on fact and is a sequel to my first book, which was published in 2005 and 2010. The storyline follows ne information I have acquired since then. As you read this book, it will become obvious why I needed to change the names of the informants. In order to make a cohesive read, I assembled the tidbits of information with times, places, and connections that are fictious. For those readers who know this issue, and/or have read Is Anybody Listening?, I'm sure you will remember where that book ends in the Jim Birchim story.

So, put on your detective hat and come along with Deborah as she tells you about the hunt for information leading to what happened to Captain James D. Birchim in the Vietnam War.

Barbara Birchim

"Oh, what tangled webs we weave when first we practice to deceive."

– Sir Walter Scott

CHAPTER ONE

My name is Deborah and I had just finished touring the Uffizi Museum in Florence, Italy, and decided I needed to have an Italian soda. I found a cute little café around the corner from the museum with small round tables and decided to order a drink from the waiter. My Italian language skills were very basic so it amazed me that he understood what I said.

Sitting outside watching the tourists and locals interact was a real treat. Everything moves at a different pace here. Nothing is fast. People enjoy looking in the windows and visiting with friends and neighbors as they stroll the windy streets.

My trip was turning out to be even better than I expected. Here I was, gazing at the rolling hills of Tuscany with its charming old towns, nestled within their surrounding walls perched on one mountain after another. As I walked into these towns with their narrow, cobblestone streets, I was taken back to the period of the Renaissance era, a time in Italy's history.

I am a detective with a task force assigned to cold cases. This work can be very frustrating. Just when I think I am getting to the answer, everything tends to dry up. So, my head was a buzz with numerous cases and trying to put the pieces together on each case. Several detectives in my office work their own multitude of cases so there's always a lot of chatter and head scratching going on all day in the office. I had found myself looking forward to my trip to Tuscany.

It's my third week of vacation and I was able to let go of work thoughts.

As I waited for my soda, two men sat down behind me. They looked like tourists as they had guidebooks in hand and cameras around their necks. Their wrinkled clothes completed their ensembles. I enjoy listening to others talk about their new experiences and as they began to speak in English, I was surprised. Something was different. The two men weren't talking about Italy. They were talking about the new information they'd just received about a man who had been missing for years. It seemed they, too, were working on a cold case.

My ears started to burn. They had been tracking information that led to this part of Italy and had decided to see if they could find any relatives of the missing person. They had been able to make a connection and some of their pieces were coming together. They were excited. Where were they going next was the question on their minds.

This opportunity was too good to pass up as one can never have enough contacts on a current cold case. I turned to them, apologized for listening to their conversation, and introduced myself. We spent the next two hours sharing ideas, facts, and contact information.

As I walked back through the narrow streets to my hotel, my mind was a buzz with the sights I had seen in this beautiful country and the new contacts I'd made that day that might help solve one of my cold cases.

I found it hard to say good-bye to Italy with all its great food and lovely people, but the time had come as I was running out of money.

CHAPTER TWO

I've always had a fascination for finding out how things tick. It used to drive my father crazy when I'd take things apart and then wouldn't put them back together again. My studies in college centered around criminal justice and foreign affairs. So, it seemed a natural fit for me to work in a department that was dedicated to finding answers to cold cases.

The building I work in has five floors, each dedicated to a different department in investigations. The first floor is the Sheriff's Department, another floor is dedicated to human trafficking cases, another for missing children, the bomb squad and potential terrorist activities are on another floor, and then there's my floor, which is dedicated to cold cases.

As I stepped off the elevator, the giant office space was buzzing with activity. I found our caseloads hadn't diminished while I was gone.

My vacation was now over and I had a renewed energy.

5

New ideas had come to mind while I was away so I started digging into my cases with a vengeance. A stack of new cases sat on my credenza, which added to all the old unsolved cold cases from the past, made for a tall pile.

One of my new cases was about an Army Special Forces and Special Operations officer who had gone Missing In Action in November 1968. This was an unusual case as my department doesn't usually take military cases, but the family had come to us as a last resort to get help. They left a copy of a book titled, "Is Anybody Listening? A True Story About The POW/MIAs In The Vietnam War," which gave all the information they had acquired throughout the years. The story revolved around a serviceman who led a team of ten men into the jungles of Laos, became surrounded by the enemy, and called for extraction by McGuire Rigs suspended below a helicopter. When the helicopter arrived back at base camp, the serviceman was not on it and the only other American on the team said the serviceman had fallen off the helicopter during the flight.

"Is Anybody Listening?" was very thorough in referencing documents and officials that were involved in the handling of the men who were listed as Prisoner of War (POW) or Missing In Action (MIA). That said, some of the leads in "Is Anybody Listening?" were left hanging, which was a good starting point for my research.

Dealing with other governmental agencies can be

difficult and the length of time for responses can be unimaginable. As a detective, I knew this wasn't going to be easy.

I had a new white board brought into my office so I could start writing the possible leads I was discovering and the direction I wanted to go. As I was doing this, one of my cohorts looked in and became interested in my case. He had been in Vietnam with the military. His name is Daniel and he served in the Army in the area of criminal investigation in Saigon during his tour. I must admit that he is a good-looking guy but you don't want to cross him. He can out run, out climb, and out fox any criminal he's after. So, the team of Deborah and Daniel, or D&D, decided they'd tackle the case together.

Within a couple of weeks, we had both read "Is Anybody Listening?" and had a long list of questions that needed answering. The main question that came to both of us was, after 53 years, why would the military be stonewalling this family? All documents should have been declassified by now so those questions that were posed years ago should be able to be answered. If this were a criminal case, the preponderance of information would lead in a different direction than the outcome that had been stated on all the documents so many years ago.

The case was not going to be an easy one for Daniel and me to solve.

CHAPTER THREE

One of the things that struck me, as I read about how family members of POWs and MIAs were treated during the Vietnam War, was that some were labeled "crazy" for information they'd received from outside military sources. Some had even claimed to have obtained hospital records of their husbands in the States, but were unable to locate the husband once he was discharged.

One family's daughter-in-law, Rebecca, had an experience that proved the serviceman was alive and wanting to make contact but seemed to be warned not to. A van selling fruits and vegetables came to the door of the daughter-in-law. She bought some produce, paid with a check, all the while thinking she recognized the man. When she said something to Joy, her mother-in-law who lived several states away, Joy sent her a picture of her missing husband. A facial recognition was made. When the check cleared the bank, it was endorsed on the back. That was sent to a handwriting expert who compared it to the missing serviceman's writing and was declared a match. The man driving the van never went back to that house and the lead ended. When all of this information was brought to the Army's Casualty Office, they did nothing. This was but one example of what those "crazy" family members were experiencing.

CHAPTER FOUR

For the next several weeks, Daniel and I came into the office shaking our heads as we continued reading "Is Anybody Listening?" and wondering why the government didn't have its own detectives working on cases like this.

Since Daniel had been in the military during the Vietnam War, he made lots of contacts while there and was now bound and determined to find those servicemen. One of them was a helicopter pilot named Pete who he knew could help answer a lot of questions in regard to aircraft and flying capabilities. This contact proved very useful. Pete reached out to the Vietnam Helicopter Pilots Association (VHPA) to try to find the crew-chief on that mission. He went even a step further and found a rigger who worked installing the McGuire Rigs on the helicopters during that period of the war. Pete asked the rigger if it was possible for two men to ride on one rig. The answer was "no." This proved it was impossible for our serviceman to have gotten on the extraction rig with the other American, so the serviceman had been left behind, no doubt about it.

This led us to the next question, which was why did the other American lie when he reported that Captain Birchim was holding on to him? Daniel and I reminded each other that Captain Birchim was on a Special Operations mission. Our country was not supposed to be in Cambodia or Laos which is where the real operation took place. For this reason, the military never declassified the mission report.

Daniel and I both agreed that once a document is written by the government, it can't be changed. We could tell that even after all these years with other documents being released and servicemen coming forward to tell what really happened, the agencies refuse to accept the new information and stand on what the original document stated. This then becomes a contest between family members and the government. Daniel and I wondered if we could have any impact on the outcome of the case we had, given this challenge.

CHAPTER FIVE

For the next few months, newspapers were carrying stories about servicemen listed as MIAs, showing-up in the States. How was that possible? Their stories were aired on national TV channels to the shock of family members. Some of them were never processed out of the military when they arrived back from Vietnam, and so were listed as MIA. Some had no families to reconnect with as parents had passed away. It wasn't until those still listed as MIA went to the Veterans Administration to get their medical benefits that even they were made aware of this discrepancy.

One interesting case was about a serviceman who left Vietnam, went to Bangkok, decided he didn't want to return to his wife in the States, so he went to Australia. This meant he never processed out of the military. He was still carried as MIA.

It wasn't until Ashley, his biological daughter in the

States, started doing research through the web that she found him. This story went viral in the news.

All of the stories we read were interesting, but Daniel and I didn't think they applied to our case. What they did prove was that the government didn't really do their detective work, and it posed the big question, how many more cases were like ours?

CHAPTER SIX

Daniel and I had put our feelers out and after a few months, information was starting to come back to us. We were getting leads which caused us to travel to different states to interview people. We spent hours on the phone and requested various agencies for information they might have on our serviceman.

One of the things we did was a Freedom of Information request to a number of the various departments—Defense Intelligence Agency, National Security Agency, Army Casualty, CIA, FBI—to name a few. We knew that as documents are declassified on a continuing basis, new information on James Birchim could have been put in that agency file. We also knew each agency had their own file system and didn't like to share information, so the odds of new information reaching Army Casualty from any of these agencies was nil.

Months passed by before all the responses came back.

The one from the CIA was quite interesting. The phrase, "We can neither confirm nor deny that we hold any information on this serviceman," made us laugh. We knew that meant they did have information but they weren't going to release it. What in the Birchim file could be considered national security?

CHAPTER SEVEN

The information pipeline started as a trickle but grew beyond our wildest dreams. Daniel and I were going to have to do some traveling to foreign countries.

Since some of our new contacts were in Thailand, it seemed like that should be our first stop. I'd have to ask Larry, the office manager, if the departments budget could handle this cost.

As we stepped off the plane in Bangkok, the heat and new smells attacked our senses. We got through customs, collected our bags, and headed for our hotel on the Chao Phraya River. Our meeting with our first contact wasn't until the next day so we had the rest of the afternoon to re-coop from the long flight.

After a short rest, we decided to go out of the hotel and do a little exploring. The population of Bangkok was about six million and I think they all had cars or tuk-tuks which were like pedi-cabs. We watched as traffic could be held at an intersection for a long time which made us realize that traffic in Los Angeles was nothing compared to this.

The humidity was high and the smells from street vendors selling food challenged our senses. Vendors sold all kinds of different things like watches, jewelry, and small leather goods. We had to pick our way through the heavy crowd, always making sure we didn't step on one of the vendors as some laid their goods on white sheets on the sidewalks.

Daniel and I decided to eat dinner at the Sheraton Hotel where we were staying. They served western style food and we didn't want to take any chances of getting an upset stomach before meeting with our contact in the morning. The view from the dining room, which overlooked the river, was stunning. Boat traffic was going up and down the river delivering people to different stops along the way, which made for an interesting form of commuter traffic.

We both retired early as tomorrow would start our hunt for more information about our case.

CHAPTER EIGHT

Early the next morning, we took a cab to our first meeting. The heat and humidity were already quite high. We were going to have to pace ourselves.

Scott, our contact, had been in the military during the Vietnam War and had taken-up residence in Thailand. We learned there were lots of retired military expats living in Thailand. Scott told us a lot about the sightings of POWs just across the border in Laos, which surprised us. He said he had lots of friends who might have pertinent knowledge on our case and after hours of talking and sharing contact information, we asked for his help. Scott was willing to reach out to his contacts and see what he could find. This had been a good day.

Back at the hotel, we made notes on everything Scott had shared with us and got ready for the next day, which was to take us to the northeast part of Thailand. This would require a plane ride early in the morning.

CHAPTER NINE

Jeff was our next contact who met us at the airport in Sakon Nakhon and took us to his house. There we met with several veterans who told us numerous stories. Nothing really seemed to pertain to our case, but could be of value later down the line in our investigation.

We stayed in that location to meet with another contact named Steve, who really opened our eyes to the possibility POWs lived just across the border. He was on-call as a translator and was kept up to date with recent movements of those prisoners.

Steve introduced us to a Thai person who was responsible for the security of one-third of the border between Thailand and Laos. We later found out that although he wore a military uniform, his role also encompassed an agency similar to our CIA. We rode along with this Thai officer who showed us one of his jungle camps, the men who staffed them, and how they operated.

By the time Daniel and I left Thailand, we had gotten so much information, we were busy the whole way back to the States on the plane. Our trip opened several avenues, which might lead to the answers we were looking for.

CHAPTER TEN

While we were gone, information had been rolling in and had created quite a pile of papers and telephone messages that needed our attention. Newspapers were running stories of MIA family members who had their loved ones' remains returned and were now asking for a DNA match as the body didn't look like their son's remains. The Central Identification Lab in Hawaii had reassured the family that the match was correct, but when an independent analysis was made, the results turned out to be different. Family members were furious. Who were they going to trust now? Was the government lab wrong or was the independent lab wrong? They thought they were closer to the truth but were they really?

Daniel and I were beginning to see we were going to be challenged from lots of different departments. Even if we got information leading in a different direction on this case, would we be able to convince the government they had made a mistake? Was this truly just a mistake or were they hiding something?

The Birchim family contacted us again with more strange evidence. They had been cleaning out their files and had come across a bundle of papers that were given to them for safe keeping. Those came from the same family who had the "vegetable man" experience. (see Chapter Three) The Birchim family contacted Joy's son who said he did want the papers and went on to tell a very strange story that had just happened. He'd received a phone call from his aunt who was the sister of the missing serviceman. She thought it was now okay to tell him that his father had just died. This was 51 years after the serviceman went missing and was then declared dead. The sister sent the obituary to Joy's son, which had a photo attached. The man's last name on the obituary was different but the photo comparison was a match. He had a family and had been living in Michigan for the past 40 years. The son was baffled as to why his dad had never made contact with him. It seems that families had heard that if any POW/MIA ever returned to the States, they were never to make contact with the family they left behind as the government wanted to keep the cover-up going. After all, at the end of the war the government declared they "left no man behind."

Before the Birchim family mailed the packet, they

looked inside and discovered sketches of Joy's husband at different ages drawn by a police artist years ago. They were a clear match to the obituary and driver's license photo of Joy's husband.

CHAPTER ELEVEN

Daniel and I had tasked our research department to go through archives looking for information about live POW/MIAs. Their findings were now creating such high stacks of newspaper clippings and documents from around the world that we had to bring in another long table.

As we read through the papers, we found articles stating the following.

> "Fifty years after World War II, three Japanese men came out of hiding on a remote section of an island in the Pacific."

> "Thirty years after the Vietnam War, 170 Hmong came out of hiding in caves. They were saying there were many more still in those caves between the Vietnam and Laos border."

> "North Korea admitted, in 2005, to holding American POWs from the Korean War. The South Korean Red Cross estimated that number could be as high as 1,031."

We found we were in the middle of a challenge to weed out pieces of information that might not pertain to our case. Our floor became littered with scraps of papers, magazines, and contacts we'd talked to which turned out not to be relevant.

Just as our brains became saturated with information about big and small fragments of this case, we received a phone call that sounded very promising. What Daniel and I heard, led us in a different direction for a while.

The information sounded strange. We needed to do some background checking on this informant which took some time but proved that we could, in fact, trust what this guy said. Once again, we discovered the time had come to go back to the family and ask more questions.

This new information all centered around payroll in Vietnam. The family remembered that in the serviceman's last letter, he had mentioned he was to be in charge of payroll for that period at his base camp. They never thought this information had anything to do with his case, so they never mentioned it to anyone.

We went back to our informant and asked if he could remember anything else. He gave us the names of two other men who might have more information. These two men were not in the same military outfits in Vietnam but had similar stories. Both had run across large stashes of shrink-wrapped U.S. monies in jungle caves.

This case had become more unbelievable by the minute.

CHAPTER TWELVE

After doing our due diligence and reconnecting with some of the contacts we'd made, we'd confirmed the information given about payroll was correct.

As Daniel had always said, "Follow the money."

What our missing serviceman discovered was that money was being skimmed off payrolls and going in different directions. He took this information to his commanding officer who was in on the scheme. As Daniel and I dug into this, we also found money came from prostitution rings, the sale of weapons, and gold. Jewels were also funneled into American hands along with drugs.

Daniel and I discovered they couldn't let our serviceman live to tell this story. After all, this went all the way to Washington, DC.

The efficient way to take care of the problem of a cover-up was to send the serviceman on a mission where he would never return.

Now we had a motive.

CHAPTER THIRTEEN

When we discovered our case was going to involve a money trail, Daniel flew into action. This was his research specialty. He targeted the names that appeared at the bottom of board reports and the names of commanding officers in 1968. It didn't take long before Daniel started finding some very odd occurrences.

For instance, how could a serviceman with little rank come back to the States and buy five pieces of property in Miami?

As Daniel went through the list of those names, he discovered this wasn't a onetime occurrence. Many persons were involved in the scheme while they were on duty in Vietnam. When they returned to their homes, which were spread-out in many States, they started buying numerous pieces of property and other very expensive items.

This operation was much bigger and more involved than we had thought and we now knew we had to stay focused on what happened to the serviceman. It seemed obvious that the Birchim would need to be removed before he went to the press or even higher authorities.

CHAPTER FOURTEEN

Another startling revelation was unfolding as we read through what the family had already tried to accomplish.

When the family felt they had made their case for the serviceman being left at the extraction site, they requested he be given the POW Medal since his men had been surrounded by the enemy and he would have been taken prisoner.

The Birchim family asked the question, "If a man is taken prisoner and died within hours, wouldn't he be deserving of the medal?"

The answer they got was, "Yes." So, the family submitted all their evidence to accomplish getting the POW Medal for James. The U.S. Army Human Resources Command was where this packet landed. Daniel and I looked at each other as we read this and thought Human Resources dealt only with live people.

In the meantime, the family contacted Army Casualty and discovered a civilian, who had been working in that office for years, knew about the request and said the status change would be happening by the end of the month. This never happened. No explanation was ever given.

Daniel and I guessed that if they had changed James Birchim's status, the Army would have to acknowledge that he was left alive at the extraction site. Then, they'd have to prove he died at another location in 1971 to cover their status change to Killed In Action Body Not Recovered (KIABNR). Afterall, "We leave no man behind."

Receiving the medal wouldn't be the only problem. If they awarded him the medal, the government would have to go back and change his pay status as he would have been kept on the active duty payrolls and would be automatically promoted in rank until he was declared dead. Those men who were declared POWs at the time of their incident, were carried as POWs till after the war in 1973.

Daniel and I discovered that all pay and allowances are stopped when a serviceman is declared Killed In Action. The widow then starts receiving Widow's Benefits which are financially less than active duty pay, and the pay grade is frozen at the rank of the serviceman at the time of his death. Birchim was declared dead in 1971 and the war ended and cases closed after 1973. Some cases weren't even closed until the late 70s.

I wondered how many other families were in this same situation.

CHAPTER FIFTEEN

We spent hours talking with helicopter pilots, servicemen who were there during the same time frame as our man, and tracking down endless leads that went nowhere.

Finally, we got access to men who were also in Special Operations. Some remembered Birchim and his story, and some were very adamant that they never left any comrade behind. When asked if they were given an order which meant they had to leave someone behind, would they do it? Reluctantly, each one of these answered "Yes." When they tried to put Daniel and me in our place about how missions were run, I asked a question I already knew the answer to.

"Were you privy to all the missions being run in Vietnam during your tour?" The answer was, "No."

"Why was that," I asked.

"Because we didn't have a need to know."

"Exactly my point," I said.

Once we got past that hurdle, we received more information on the terrain in that area and the feelings of those in Special Ops assigned to that base camp. This was building even more evidence that we were on the right track.

We needed another white board.

CHAPTER SIXTEEN

One of our new contacts had been working hard to find pieces of information we needed as some of the men we contacted wouldn't talk to us. When Daniel introduced himself to them as a Vietnam Veteran, this made a difference. When information came from a non-English speaking person, it became even more difficult because we were afraid that something might get lost in translation.

We had to be very careful not to get our hopes up on information coming from only one direction. The more times we heard the same information coming from different directions, the more confident we were that the information was accurate.

Daniel and I approached cold cases like doing a jigsaw puzzle. The hard copy evidence became the border. As fragments of the case came in, we tried to match them with other pieces. If they were new, they stayed by themselves outside the perimeter. Our puzzle still had some large holes but they were filling-in day-by-day. A picture was forming and what we were seeing wasn't a very nice one.

CHAPTER SEVENTEEN

Information began to come in from Thailand. Time to pack a suitcase for another trip.

After a long plane ride, several airline meals, a commuter flight, and a couple of airports, we arrived at our destination in the northeast part of Thailand.

This time Daniel and I were meeting with a new contact, named Alex, who'd also seen the photos of our serviceman. Daniel and I were really hoping the information this time would pan out.

As we drank Thai tea in a small café, the story of the recognition was told to us by our new friend. It seems he had seen the man we sought in a bakery farther north some months before. At that time, Alex didn't think anything about the Caucasian man being there as many retired Americans were living in the area. We asked if he would take us to the bakery so we could find this mystery man.

The answer was, "Yes."

Our plans were to drive to the area the next day. We were anxious to meet the mystery American.

CHAPTER EIGHTEEN

The morning was hot and steamy as we got into our van with our new friend for the ride north in Thailand. We passed rice paddies where farmers plowed with oxen. Other areas we drove through had dense foliage. Some of the houses had a western look and others were more primitive. People were walking on the side of the road heading toward open-air markets to get their food for the day and others were riding their bicycles, which were loaded with things to sell. We were hopeful to make contact with the man in our picture.

Our new friend went into the bakery and came out with a smile. The person we were looking for had been in that morning. The bakery lady had even given Alex directions to this man's house. Off we went.

How we found the place, I don't know. We exited the main road and proceeded on a dirt road for about a mile. Then we turned right at a big rock, which we did find, and a left at the next bifurcation. The dirt road ended and then we had to walk to the house that couldn't be seen from where we had to park.

When the owner of the house came out to greet us, Daniel and I knew this wasn't our man. His features were similar but because we'd had an aging picture done of our serviceman, we were sure he wasn't Birchim. However, our conversation with him gave us lots of information. It seems he had flown with Air America during the war. Bingo! CIA! Daniel and I both knew that once you're a CIA person, you're always a CIA person for the rest of your life. We gave little information but got a lot. This man's interest and knowledge in a specific science was exactly the same as our serviceman's. How bizarre. He also mentioned knowing a person at the National Academy of Science in San Francisco. Birchim had co-authored a technical paper with the same person before entering the Army. What are the odds? When we asked him if he knew anyone else living in the area with an interest in this field, he refused to say. Gotcha!

What an exciting day. Our conversation in the van on the way back to our hotel was full of hope that we had made some real progress. We knew the man interviewed would be talking to his friends who would spread the word about our quest for answers.

Our question was, why did this man clam-up when

we asked if he knew an entomologist in the area? What was he hiding? Was our serviceman possibly working for the CIA?

We were going to need another white board.

CHAPTER NINETEEN

Getting back to work was difficult as our heads were buzzing with the information we had acquired and possible directions we now needed to go. However, that would have to wait as we were confronted with stacks of new mail and messages that had come in during our trip to Thailand.

First, I needed to call the Birchim family, let them know what we had discovered on our trip, and ask them some questions, which came to us as we talked with our mysterious contact. Sometimes families don't intentionally withhold information from those working on their cold case, but a tiny detail might be what glues the trails together.

One of the questions to the Birchim family was, had they given a DNA sample to the government? If we found James alive, we could then verify him by matching his sample with the family's sample. The family was curious as to why we would even ask this. Our thoughts went to three possibilities.

1) He was alive and didn't want to be found, in which case we'd have to collect DNA from something he left behind.

2) He didn't know he was James Birchim and we could ask for a sample from him so we could run a match. 3) If he had been living under another name and passed away, maybe we could get a DNA sample from his bones.

We were way ahead of ourselves, at this point, in asking for DNA samples, but something about our recent Air America contact in Thailand struck us as most odd. The way he completely shut down when we asked if he knew any other entomologists in the area was suspicious. As detectives, we have learned to listen to our gut and what we felt was our man could possibly be alive.

We decided to call together the whole team of cold case detectives in our office to outline our case and get some feedback as to whether or not Daniel and I had gotten off track. What we discovered was there were many more veterans in our midst who were interested and eager to help. The detectives were helping us by making suggestions, which we put on yet another white board. We were so pleased to get their ideas on pursuing our case.

By the end of the day, I was frazzled. All I wanted to do was to go home, soak in a hot tub, and have a glass of wine.

CHAPTER TWENTY

There's an old adage I remembered -- Your home is your safe haven. Over the years, that's come into question for me as some of the cases I've worked on have brought unwelcome visitors to my front door. With the advent of all these new kinds of electronic gizmos, I now have cameras angled all around my property which allows me to decide if I want to open the front door or not. This does put my mind at rest to some extent.

I live in a quiet community with lovely neighbors who watch out for each other. Our holiday parties are fun as there's always lots of good food, drinks, and laughs. The only one that doesn't enjoy the holidays is my cat. Lucy is a calico who has been with me for almost four years. She's a one-person cat who really doesn't like other people or noisy events. The Fourth of July is the worst for her. She takes three days to come out of hiding once the fireworks end.

Gardening is one of the things that takes me away

from all the questions at work. Something about planting and tidying-up the fallen leaves makes me feel good.

All the distractions come to an end every Monday morning when I walk back into my office.

CHAPTER TWENTY-ONE

Everyone was drinking coffee and planning their attack on their cases for the next five days, which meant the chatter was at a minimum.

I watched as Daniel seemed to drag himself over to his desk. He looked like he'd either had a rough weekend or he was slightly hungover. Hard to tell. His hair was going in all directions and his shirt looked lived-in. Maybe, he was really recovering from a very good weekend. I knew that he wasn't married, but did have a rather steady girlfriend as he'd showed me a picture of a cute blond. She worked in a museum as a curator, so the two of them probably had some interesting conversations. I think museum talk wasn't the only thing on their mind.

My phone started ringing, which brought me back to reality. My boss, Larry, wanted to see me. He wanted an update on my case and informed me numerous phone messages were waiting for me at the reception desk.

CHAPTER TWENTY-TWO

As I went through the phone messages, one of them stood out. I recognized John's name as he was a contact, we'd been given months ago, who didn't have much to tell us. I wondered what was on his mind, now. I settled into my chair and dialed his number.

John started telling me about someone in Costa Rica who had some information we needed to hear. John wouldn't say what the information was because we had to hear it "straight from the horse's mouth."

It looked like my week was starting off with a bang.

As I looked at the case files piling up on my desk, I decided some of them had to go to other detectives. I went back to Larry to ask if this could be done. He wrinkled-up his face, shook his head, and told me who had the smallest case load.

Harry gave me a nasty look when I dropped ten cases on his desk. I apologized and backed away.

I heard the phone in my office and ran to get it. John was confirming his friend had information on Birchim.

Now, I needed to approach Daniel about our taking and funding a trip to Costa Rica to meet Steve, our new contact there. The time had arrived for us to get our calendars together and figure out what dates would work for each of us. Then, I needed to get back to John to make sure his contact would be around when we arrived. Daniel and I decided we'd each take some vacation days during this trip as neither of us had ever been to this part of the world. By the end of the day, we'd formalized our plans, made our flight arrangements, and booked a hotel. As I dropped Daniel's tickets on his desk, he looked up at me and asked what kind of attire this trip would need. I told him to nix the Hawaiian print shirts and stick with very warm weather clothes.

Now I needed to find a cat sitter for Lucy.

CHAPTER TWENTY-THREE

Costa Rica is a beautiful country. Our flight took us to San Jose, a city with a mixture of Spanish and western styles. As we landed, I hoped my high school Spanish would come back. Steve, our new contact there, had given me his address and instructions to take a taxi to a community a couple of miles out of town. We saw lush green vegetation and tropical flowers growing along the road. Off in the distance we could see the volcano I'd read about in a travel magazine. It had been dormant for years and I was hoping we wouldn't see it come alive while we were there.

The address led us to a white-washed casita with red hibiscus flowers growing around the windows. As we walked up the dirt path toward the door, I wondered what kind of information we were going to get since we hadn't received any hints before we left.

The door stood open as we approached the casita. Standing in front of us was an American I guessed to be about 65 years old. He obviously knew who we were as he greeted us and introduced himself as Steve. He welcomed us into his bright living room decorated in reds and yellows. As I gazed around the room, I noticed a painting titled, "Self Portrait with a Thorn Necklace," done by the artist Frida Kahlo from Mexico. Small pottery bowls, fresh cut flowers, and a beautiful woven rug with a Mayan design added to the décor of the room. A tray with lemonade, iced tea, and glasses sat on a dining room table along with some small appetizers. Steve said to help ourselves while he left to get his wife. Daniel and I smiled at each other while we filled our glasses and found a place to sit down.

As we waited for Steve to return, we could see the backyard through the sliding glass doors on the other side of the dining table. The doors were open allowing us to watch a large parrot swinging outside the door while he talked to someone. The someone was Steve's wife, Flower, who had been gardening when Steve found her to tell her the guests had arrived.

We stood as she entered the room and were somewhat surprised as a Vietnamese lady stood before us.

She smiled and said, "My name is hard to pronounce so everyone calls me Flower."

"What a pretty name," I said.

Steve got the two of them some iced tea and then suggested we go out on the back veranda to talk.

He started the conversation by telling us about his having been in the Vietnam War, where he had been stationed, and what his assignment had been. He had shared a small apartment in Saigon with another man in his unit and Flower used to do the cleaning and cooking for them. By the time his 15-month tour was over, they had become close and Steve wanted to bring Flower back to the States. She had a hard time with the idea because she would have to leave all of her relatives behind. At last, she agreed to marry Steve and leave Vietnam.

I was beginning to get hopeful Flower was going to reveal some pertinent information on Birchim. What did she know? Who did she know? Where was this going?

Just then, their parrot started squawking. He was really making a fuss and our attention got diverted to what made him do this. Then we saw it. A big cat had jumped on to the table near the parrot's swing. The two of them had a real hissing and squawking fest for several minutes. Flower and Steve just watched and smiled. I guessed this was a regular occurrence.

"When did you leave Vietnam?" I said to Flower.

"We left in seventy-three and went to Australia for two years. Then, Steve's friend in Costa Rica said this would be a peaceful place to live out our lives so we decided to move."

I said to Flower, "I'm sure Steve told you about our Birchim case and that we were trying to find answers for his family. Steve thought you might have some information that could help us."

Flower nodded. "This is a rather long story. Would you like to refresh your drinks before I start?"

We all walked to the dining table, refilled our glasses, and ate a couple of the nachos, pieces of cheese, and some guava-strawberries-oranges that were on sticks. "These are delicious. How do you make the nacho dip?" I asked.

"The nachos are my mother's favorite recipe and I've been sworn not to give it out," Flower replied.

"If she ever decides to let you share that recipe, please send it to me."

We made our way back to the comfortable seating arrangement in the living room area.

I wanted to be as open about what we were doing as possible so I asked, "Do you mind if I take notes while you talk?"

"I don't mind at all," Flower replied.

As Flower began her story, I could tell I was going to be busy writing down a string of events, times, and places. I wished I'd brought my mini-recorder with me.

"My cousin was a poor farmer on the border between

Cambodia and Laos in nineteen sixty-eight. At that time, the North Vietnamese Army had a large number of men all over the area."

"It must have been difficult for him to tend his crops," I said.

"The Americans, along with the South Vietnamese Army, would send patrols into the same area to watch the movement of the enemy. My cousin had to be very careful when he'd go into the woods to hunt for food because he might run across these factions fighting."

Flower stopped for a minute and took a sip of tea.

"One day he heard a helicopter overhead and watched as it got closer and closer to the tree tops."

Daniel asked, "Did your cousin say what time of the day he heard this?"

"He didn't mention if it was in the morning or afternoon. My brother did say the helicopter dropped ropes and he could see men were attaching themselves to the ropes and being pulled up and away. There were three ropes and three men, each on his own rope. The gun fire didn't stop so my cousin crawled up to an overlook point to see what was going on. There was one Army man that had been left behind."

Daniel said, "Did your cousin mention whether or not the man had injuries?"

"He couldn't tell, but the enemy surrounded the serviceman and took him away."

All of a sudden, there was a knock at the door. Steve went to see who it was and while he was gone, I asked Flower about the Frida Kahlo painting.

"Where did you find that wonderful painting by Frida?"

"Steve and I went to Mexico for a short vacation and visited an art gallery in San Miguel de Allende. They had so many beautiful paintings by her that it was hard to decide which one we wanted. This one was the one we liked and could afford."

Steve came back in the room and said, "It was the paper boy collecting for this month's subscription. Did I miss anything?"

"I was just telling them about our painting and where we purchased it," Flower said.

We got back to the Birchim case.

"Several months after my cousin's first sighting," Flower said, "he was again foraging for food only this time he was on the Cambodian side of the border. He knew there was a hospital run by the North Vietnamese in the area so he had to be careful. As he came over a ridge, he saw the structure. He watched for a while and saw people moving about outside."

I interrupted Flower and said, "Your command of

the English language is very good. Did you go to school when you were in Australia and take English as a second language?"

"Actually, it's my third language. We spoke French and Vietnamese when I was growing up."

"I'm very impressed as I can only speak English. Please go on with your story."

Flower continued. "My cousin said there were guards walking around the compound and military men carrying wounded soldiers inside the hospital. Outside one of the side doors, patients were sitting or lying in the sun. He recognized one of those men as the man who had been left behind that day when the helicopters flew away. The man looked in rough shape and had a bandage around his head and one on his leg. My cousin thought he was the only Caucasian in that group. He never went back to the area but heard a few years later the hospital had been abandoned."

Daniel asked her some questions he had about anything else her cousin might have seen during the 1968-1972 timeframe. He was trying to corroborate her cousin's information with what he knew.

My questions were about the physical characteristics of the man she told us about. Flower was only able to remember her cousin saying the man wasn't very tall and had light brown hair.

Steve, too, said he had heard about the initial incident of a man listed as "missing" when he was in Saigon, but because of the Special Ops mission, no other information was available.

We had spent the entire afternoon talking until we'd decided we should take our leave. They invited us to stay for dinner, but we declined as we needed to return to San Jose for our midnight flight back to the States. Daniel expressed our grateful appreciation for the information they had given us and asked them to contact us if they remembered anything else.

Almost the entire trip home to California was spent in silence as Daniel and I processed the amazing story we had just heard.

Our jigsaw puzzle of information would have some pieces, which we could fit together, but many of them would not be within the border of our puzzle.

CHAPTER TWENTY-FOUR

Lucy was at the front door scolding me as I arrived home. I could see she had been up to her old tricks while I was away for several things had been moved around and pillows from the couch were on the floor. The teenager who lived next-door had been feeding her and cleaning her box, but hadn't cleaned-up any of the messes left from kitty litter or water. Time to pay some attention to Lucy.

The weekend was upon me and so were the usual chores. A good thing they didn't take much thought as my mind was elsewhere.

The information Flower had given us kept running through my head on a continuous loop. I needed to get back to "Is Anybody Listening?" to see if anything in the book fit what we'd just discovered. I was almost positive I hadn't read about a hospital.

Could it be that the enemy had taken James Birchim prisoner? But would they do that? One of Daniel's friends had told us the enemy would usually kill wounded soldiers if they caught them. Why would Birchim be different?

I carried my cleaning tools upstairs and headed to my office. When I opened the door, I noticed this wasn't the way I left it before going to Costa Rica.

The papers on top of my desk had been scattered around and the desk drawers were open. The drawers in the file cabinet had not been closed completely and my office chair had been moved over to my computer stand. All of this was giving me a creepy feeling.

I phoned the cat sitter to see if she knew anything about this. She told me she hadn't been upstairs and didn't see anyone going into my house while I was away.

I decided to take some pictures of this mess so I could show Daniel on Monday.

What was someone looking for?

Everything that had been pulled out of my file cabinet had been about the Birchim case. Even though I had other case files sitting on my desk, those hadn't been touched. Why would someone break into my house to see what kind of information I had on the Birchim case? Could it be the government? Why would they care if Daniel and I found Jim Birchim either alive or dead? This made no sense.

I finished straightening the office and cleaning the

upstairs, and decided I needed a cup of tea. I needed to think.

If someone is interested in knowing what I know about the Birchim case, why don't they just ask me? Breaking into my house while I'm gone shows "they" are desperate. My stomach was starting to turn into knots. If "they" would break into my house, what else might "they" try?

In the police academy, we were taught several techniques for surveillance, for not being followed, and for how to lose someone who is chasing you. It was time for me to refresh myself on these techniques.

I found it hard to go to sleep Saturday night because I kept thinking about the possibility of someone breaking in. For the first time in many years, I placed my service revolver on the night stand.

Why I felt safer with Lucy next to me I don't know, but I did.

Sunday morning was beautiful but the intruder was still on my mind. I decided to call Daniel and tell him what had happened. Maybe the same thing happened to him.

Daniel realized that I was shaken by all of this and came over after his Sunday jog. I showed him the pictures I'd taken of my office yesterday. He, too, was puzzled. He suggested I go to a hotel to get a good night's sleep. I felt like his idea wasn't going to solve my problem. I needed to be more devious than the intruder.

A light bulb went on in my head.

Daniel and I started setting-up cameras and audio recording equipment hidden in various places around the inside of the house. We also installed new outside cameras and a doorbell that alerted me to any sound or movement.

I was beginning to feel safer.

CHAPTER TWENTY-FIVE

The office was a buzz of activity as I walked in Monday morning. High-fives were going around for those cases being closed. Papers were being distributed, people were getting coffee, and a general sense of chaos prevailed. A herd of men raced toward me waving their hands when they noticed me. It seems contacts had been made on my case, which might prove to be helpful and all the Veterans felt duty-bound to help. I listened to each man, took notes, and told them I'd give a briefing on Daniel's and my trip in the next day or two.

At one point in time, I had sent requests to several government agencies for information that could be released under the Freedom of Information Act. Now, sitting on my desk, were responses from the Defense Intelligence Agency and the FBI. Some archive material I'd requested had also arrived. Since Daniel hadn't gotten any phone calls while we were gone, I handed him the stack sitting on my desk.

What I saw surfacing were repeated stories about families and outsiders being harassed who were interested in the POW/MIA issue. Even Monika Jensen-Stevenson, who was a co-producer for the TV show "60 Minutes," felt she had to move her family to Canada to be safe because she was being physically threatened for delving into the POW/MIA issue. For some reason, the government didn't want anyone to start digging into information that might lead to answers. The more information I got, the more I realized recurring themes kept happening. They could be physical or psychological. The evidence was staring me in the face, so it was time to make separate lists of our bits and pieces of evidence.

I wonder how many white boards can fit in my office.

CHAPTER TWENTY-SIX

My lists were starting to take shape as I placed each piece of evidence in a separate column.

My way of accepting authenticity was to have the same information coming from at least three sources and those sources not be related. For instance, everyone who gave us information agreed Jim was in Vietnam in 1968. The columns with only one piece of information were suspect. I would need to do more digging so I could count those pieces as viable.

Flower had given us information no one else had. How was I going to verify any of that? Could I possibly find one of the soldiers who took Jim prisoner? My brain was reeling as I tried to think of a possible avenue leading me to the North Vietnamese cadre.

The time to give the office my update briefing arrived.

With everyone circled around my many white boards and columns of information, ideas started flowing.

Had we contacted the Special Forces or the Special Operations Associations?

Was there any information from the National Security Agency in our materials? Maybe they could answer questions about troop movement.

Had we looked at the debriefs of the returned POWs? Maybe they saw something or crossed paths with Jim. This was a great idea, but we found those reports were classified and therefore a dead-end unless we could find someone to look for us.

One of the other detectives said he had an acquaintance who had been a North Vietnam soldier and he would ask him for help. Wow! I almost jumped out of my chair for this sounded very hopeful.

The suggestions and questions went on for about 30 minutes. Some of the questions we could answer but those answers then led to more questions. Our meeting was very productive.

After a long day, I needed to decompress. Lucy and I both needed to be fed. She got the cat food and I fixed pasta. There's nothing more soothing that a big bowl of pasta and a glass of wine at the end of the day. We both got on the sofa and started to watch the National Geographic Channel on TV. The shows are about archeology sites in exotic places, which is interesting to me. I can escape from my office work and become engrossed in a different topic. However, tonight was different.

The first part of the hour-long show was dedicated to finding any anomalies in the ground. They were using Lidar, also known as laser scanning, to see what was beneath the terrain. It showed structures that had been buried for hundreds of years.

The second half of the show talked about the use of DNA to help identify ancient bones. Through this technology, they were able to determine the specimen they were looking at came from the family line of a great pharaoh.

I was glued to the TV.

This meant, if we could get a bone fragment from Jim's extraction site, DNA sequencing could tell us if it belonged to him.

I needed to find out if the government had ever gone to that site to investigate.

Lucy didn't seem interested in the show. I guess tomorrow night we'll have to watch Animal Planet.

CHAPTER TWENTY-SEVEN

Where was Daniel? He always greeted me with a cup of coffee when I arrived at work but he wasn't there this morning. Taped to my phone was a note from him reminding me he was taking some vacation days and would be back on the following Monday. As I surveyed my office space, I realized I'd have plenty to keep me busy until he returned.

The long string of emails took me several hours to go through. Some had interesting pieces of information and others had possible leads. I was also getting suggestions to read some books written on the topic of MIAs and POWs. It looked like I needed to do some ordering from the Amazon Corporation before Lucy and I enjoyed watching Animal Planet tonight.

The more I worked on this case, the clearer it became that men were left behind at the end of the Vietnam War. I had already read "Kiss The Boys Good-bye" written by Monica Jensen-Stevenson and "An Enormous Crime" by former Representative Bill Hendon who talked about this, which confirmed the government documents I had in my possession. Yet, officials said, leaving men behind never happened. Oh, sure, there were a couple of brave congressmen who continued to fight for the return of live prisoners and information on the location of remains, but our government never got behind the effort. Was this because "we" didn't want to go back to war with Vietnam over the issue? Or, did "we" want to keep the dirty laundry hidden? I was pondering these questions when Larry walked into my office and reminded me, we were having a lunch meeting in fifteen minutes.

Larry, my boss, started the meeting by giving all of us information on a couple of new cold cases he had just received. When he finished, we each gave updates on the cases we were working on. Some of the detectives had made real progress and others were at a dead-end. Often times, we needed to put a case aside for weeks, months, or even years before new leads came to us. These cases were never forgotten or placed in a dusty file cabinet, but rather reviewed at least every six months. I wondered if the government ever reviewed their cases and if Birchim was one of them.

The five o'clock bell rung for me to get away from my office computer and go home.

For some reason, my mind was on Chinese food. I'd need to remember to order some extra crispy noodles as Lucy loved them.

CHAPTER TWENTY-EIGHT

You have to love ordering books online through Amazon. The books I had ordered arrived in two days and I almost needed a crane to get them into my house. Ye gods. I had a lot of reading to do.

What I discovered as I went from book to book, was a lot of the same information being given. Some were eye witness accounts and other information was second-hand. One account was from a civilian POW who had been held for over five years in jungle camps. What struck me about this particular account was I hadn't seen any other information on a civilian or any other POW being held in jungle camps for that length of time. This made me realize the possibility of someone surviving under extreme conditions. That meant, Birchim could still be alive.

The information I was collecting from these books was now going under each specific column on the white boards in my office. Credibility was building on many of the points that both the Birchim family and other resources had given me.

I couldn't wait till Daniel's return to fill him in on everything.

CHAPTER TWENTY-NINE

A steaming cup of coffee was waiting for me as I entered my office on Monday morning. Hurrah! Daniel was back.

He filled me in on his fantastic surfing holiday in Mexico and told me about every meal he ate. The food sounded delicious and was starting to make me hungry for a breakfast burrito.

I, in turn, filled him in on all the new developments in the Birchim case. His eyes were starting to glaze-over as I showed him the white boards that had been updated and the string of columns I'd made of like information.

"What do you see now forming on this case?"

Daniel thought about it. I could tell his brain was trying to catch-up with what he saw in front of him. Each piece of information was like a building block to him. He now was stacking the new pieces where they belonged and it took a few minutes before he spoke. "It's hard for me to believe our government would be so callous. To knowingly

79

leave soldiers behind, is beyond my comprehension. How could they keep this such a secret?"

I replied, "It's called compartmentalization. The fewer people who know, the smaller number of people you have to control."

Daniel thought about that and shook his head.

I said, "The government also has time on their side as men who came back are dying from Agent Orange or old age and the younger generation doesn't know anything about what really happened during that war. Daniel, if this kind of behavior isn't stopped it will continue to permeate the very core of what this country stands for. I know we can't undo all of what's been done to our veterans who are unaccounted for, but we've got to get closure for at least this one case."

The rest of the day, Daniel was busy sorting through the papers and phone messages on his desk. I could tell he was deep in thought over what I'd shared with him. I wondered if he might be interested in some of the books I ordered from Amazon.

CHAPTER THIRTY

I found a message from Pete, my helicopter contact, on my desk when I arrived at the office the next morning. He needed to talk to me ASAP.

"Pete, how are you?"

"I'm fine. I was talking with some helicopter buddies about the case you're working. They asked me if I knew about thermal imagining ground-penetrating radar. It seems one of my friends has used it to find a lost cemetery in Ecuador. It worked so well that they could see every single grave in the area they were working. The more they told me about this, the more I thought it might help you with your case. If your man was left behind and buried at that site, this kind of radar should be able to detect those remains."

"Thank you so much, Pete, for sharing this information. I'm definitely going to see if the government is using this and if not, why not. I think the biggest hurdle we have right now is getting to that site."

"If you need some help, let me know. My friends are willing to fly you into the site in Southeast Asia if it is allowable."

"You may regret that offer."

CHAPTER THIRTY-ONE

Working cold cases can be frustrating. Just when you get some momentum going, everything stops. Months and even years can go by before another lead shows up. Daniel and I had cleared our desks of information on the Birchim case. The only thing staring us in the face were the white boards filled with Birchim information and the columns of like testimonies we'd gotten from leads. Now it was a waiting game.

The FOIA requests had come back but there was no new information in the documents the various agencies had sent us.

Since we got this case, the government was sending more teams in to various crash sites and finding remains of missing servicemen, so our hope was that our case would be considered for investigation the following year. These sites are planned years in advance and the Birchims were hoping, after 53 years of waiting, their case would be on the top of the review pile.

I did have other cases to keep me busy but my thoughts were always on the Birchim file. My biggest frustration with this case was the lack of sharing information between each agency involved with this issue. No one agency, even Army Casualty, had a complete file on Birchim. How could they even hope to accomplish finding any of the missing men? I had also discovered each MIA family was responsible to contact each agency and request the information they held, then piece together a complete file on their serviceman. This had to be done on a regular basis as classified documents were being declassified daily which might pertain to their case.

Since our department deals with people who have gone missing, I've seen some families go through different stages of dealing with not having answers to their questions. It's like the stages of death-and-dying only there's no death to end it all. So, these families go back and forth through the stages continuously. This means, we never know how they will react to information we might give them. Most of the time, they are very appreciative for new information. That said, new information is like ripping a scab off a wound. The agony on their faces shows us how raw that wound still is.

Daniel and I were getting ready to go home when he came into my office.

"Can you come over to my place now? There's something I want to show you."

I'd never been to his place and was a little curious to see what it looked like.

"I'd love to. Let me turn-off my computer and put a couple of things away. I'll follow you to your place in five minutes."

During the drive, my mind conjured up a picture of dishes in his sink, clothes strewn around on the floor, and general clutter everywhere. Isn't that how bachelors live?

Daniel had a cute little cottage with a white picket fence around it. I loved the red front door as it gave the crisp white paint on the exterior of his place a real pop of color. As I walked to the door, I noticed the various flowers around the foundation of the house, which were all in full bloom and realized that Daniel must have a green thumb or a great gardener. When we got inside, I was amazed. His place was neat as a pin and decorated in a beachy theme. Jars of sea shells sat in various places. A mermaid clock hung on the wall. I guess I shouldn't have been surprised at that for I knew he loved to surf, which meant he loved the beach.

"Would you like a glass of wine? I have a chardonnay and a merlot. Which would you prefer?"

"That merlot sounds really good."

After he filled our glasses, we went back to the living room and sat down.

"You know I was in the Army for a few years. Several friends reenlisted for a couple more tours in Afghanistan. There's someone I want you to meet."

Daniel left the room and came back with a big dog. It was a Belgian Malinois.

"My friend Rick was a dog handler in Afghanistan. Rick got badly wounded and will be in rehab for many months. I said I'd take care of the dog until he got home. The dog's name is Rip and he's highly trained to sniff-out bombs and people. I was wondering if he could sniff-out buried cadavers. When I asked Rick that question, he said it wouldn't take much training for Rip since he already knew how to find live people using his nose."

I knew what Daniel was thinking.

"If we could get to the Birchim site in Laos, maybe Rip could find the body. That's if Birchim was buried there."

"Do you think Rick would allow us to use his dog?"

"He'd be proud to have Rip working to bring a fallen soldier home."

"Now, we have to find a way to get to that site."

CHAPTER THIRTY-TWO

The time had arrived for me to start asking the government if they were using cadaver dogs and the two types of radar I'd heard about. I tried getting those answers by phoning a couple of different departments and agencies I thought would have the answers, but never got any confirmations either way. In desperation, I went back to the Birchim family and asked if, by chance, they knew. It turned out, they had just returned from Washington, DC, and the yearly government briefings on MIAs.

Barbara said, "For the past three years, I brought up that suggestion of using Lidar Radar at the Q & A session and told them it was being used successfully to find hidden objects by archeologists in Egypt. The panel said it couldn't be used and really made me feel like some kind of an idiot.

"This year, the panel proudly gave a presentation on how they were using Lidar Radar in Southeast Asia to find crash sites. I wanted to scream.

"As to the use of infrared radar, I can ask Army Casualty and let you know what they say."

Barbara continued, "Another family asked the question about the use of cadaver dogs at the Q & A session and the government hadn't thought of that and were going to look in to using them. We, family members, guess we'll have to wait until next year to find out whether or not that will really happen."

"It sounds like the government is finally getting up to speed with the technology that's available for both finding and identifying sites and remains," I said.

"It's better than it was even ten years ago, but families have to continuously challenge them to update their technologies and their out-of-the-box thinking. We are the ones who have to bring the new ideas to their attention. Once done, we will have to make sure they do something with those ideas. The whole process is exhausting," Barbara replied.

"Our office is always open to you. Call anytime with questions or suggestions for possible leads and I'll do the same."

CHAPTER THIRTY-THREE

The week was moving slowly on all my cases. This always makes me antsy. I start questioning whether I'd forgotten to follow-up on something which could be the reason why the phone wasn't ringing or there weren't any messages on my desk.

Outside, the city was under a thick blanket of fog which didn't help my mood. Maybe a strong cup of coffee would lift my spirits. I headed to the office kitchen where I met some of the other detectives who were also getting their morning java fix. There was talk about what went on over the weekend, who mowed their lawn, who had done home repairs and what kind of products they used. I couldn't chime in on any of this as I had been on my sofa with Lucy the whole weekend binge watching some new series on Netflix.

As I walked back to my office, I noticed that Daniel was on the phone and very animated. He was feverishly taking notes when he saw me heading his way. He waved at me as he ended his conversation and I could tell he had something he wanted to share with me.

"I've got a new lead and it sounds very promising. A man by the name of Ben saw our request for information on Birchim in a magazine and was calling to say he wanted to talk to us. He's a veteran and lives in Chicago. It sounds like he's got some new information but he doesn't want to talk about it on the phone. I can clear my calendar, can you?"

It sounded like it was time for another road trip.

CHAPTER THIRTY-FOUR

Two motel nights, multiple meals, four tanks of gas, and two thousand miles later we were ready to meet Ben.

Word was getting around, through various veteran groups, that we were trying to find answers to our questions about Captain Birchim, which led Ben to us. He had tracked down our phone number and hoped the information he had might help. He was a financial planner with a large firm and asked us to meet him at his office in downtown Chicago.

As we stepped off the elevator on the fifth floor of his building, we realized Ben's firm took up the entire floor. A lady, behind the large carved wood reception desk, greeted us and asked how she could help us. When we told her we had an appointment to see Ben, she called him and then ushered us back to his very impressive office with full length windows overlooking the city. After introducing ourselves and giving Ben a little background on what we already knew about the case, Ben started talking.

"I was in Vietnam in 1968 and was attached to a Bright Light team. We were sent in to find and bring back downed pilots or any serviceman that didn't come back from their mission. I remember the Birchim incident. My team wasn't on-call that evening. The next morning at our briefing, we were updated on what happened the previous day. The odd thing was that no team was sent in to find Birchim. Everyone in the room thought this was more than odd. Someone asked if he had made it back on his own but the answer was, no. I asked if we were going to send in a team today. Again, the answer was no.

"We knew that Birchim was being extracted in Laos, a classified area, but we had missions in classified areas all the time. However, something was not right."

He stopped, was quiet, and turned towards the windows. It looked like he was reliving that time and place. We sat quietly waiting for him to continue. When he turned back towards us, we could tell this was emotional for him as his eyes were a little red.

"We had a pub in our compound where we would meet at the end of the day and had beers. Birchim's case was the talk at each table and on each bar stool that evening. No one could understand why a Bright Light team wasn't sent in to find him. A couple of weeks after the incident, a board was convened and an official written report made about what had happened. One of my buddies typed that report and showed it to me. There were huge errors in it. For instance, the report said Birchim had been extracted using a McGuire Rig by holding on to the back of another American for 30-45 minutes before falling off the rig."

He stopped, sighed, and turned his head toward the floor while he reached for a Kleenex in his pocket.

"The report gave the map coordinates of where Birchim could possibly have fallen, which was deep inside Vietnam and north of the landing strip in Kontum."

Ben continued, "We all looked at each other in total disbelief. First of all, a McGuire Rig couldn't hold two men. Secondly, Birchim couldn't have held on that long even if he hadn't been wounded, which he was. Thirdly, the helicopter's fuel tank didn't hold enough fuel to fly the route the report said it did. What the hell was going on with this case? I never heard another word about Birchim."

"Ben, do you want to take a break?" I asked.

"Let me get some water from the mini bar behind you. Do either of you want some?" Ben asked. He grabbed three bottles and placed two in front of Daniel and me.

Ben started again. "When it came to my attention that you were trying to find information on Birchim, I contacted all my buddies to see if they had heard anything on him since 1968. The answer was no. Birchim's incident has been buried and no one knows why."

Our meeting with Ben went on for two hours. We

posed questions to try and clarify some of the ways military operations were handled during 1968. As we talked, more and more questions came to mind. Since Daniel had been in the Army, he understood a lot more of what Ben was sharing than I did.

Over dinner, Daniel and I discussed what Ben had said. We were both struck by the fact that even Ben and his buddies thought something was strange in the handling of the Birchim incident.

During our drive back to California, there were periods of total silence while we each tried to refit this Birchim jigsaw puzzle in our heads. I could now put a few more pieces inside the border, but the problem was, new single pieces of information were appearing each time we talked to a new contact.

CHAPTER THIRTY-FIVE

Lucy greeted me at the door when I arrived back from my trip to Chicago. I knew that I wouldn't be able to get anything done with all the meowing that was coming from her. She needed some attention so I put my things down and headed to the kitchen to get some dinner for the two of us. She had finished her Meow Mix cat food in a flash so I put the TV on to entertain her while I made a salad and sandwich for myself. The meowing continued and I could tell that if I wanted time to eat, the Animal Planet program needed to be on to entertain Lucy.

Because of the time difference between Chicago and the West Coast, I was up early the next morning. A hot steamy shower was calling me as I made my way to the bathroom. I loved my newly remodeled bathroom. The soft blue-green ocean colors made any tensions in my body dissolve. Inside the shower, I had one of those big square shower heads installed along with some jets that sprayed from the side walls. When the water was on full blast, it was almost like getting a massage. I did some of my best thinking just standing and being pelted for twenty minutes. My mind drifted as the water cascaded down my body and then it hit me. I had an idea for the Birchim case. I dried off, patted Lucy on the head, and headed to work.

CHAPTER THIRTY-SIX

"Daniel, I had an idea this morning and I want to run it by you. Have you got a minute?"

"Let me get some coffee and I'll be right with you."

Getting coffee sounded like a good plan so I followed Daniel into the break room and added a little cream and sugar to top-off my brew. I'll worry about calories tomorrow.

I pulled my contact list as Daniel entered my office.

"Remember the case a few years ago in Denver, about the lady who went missing around Christmas time? The detectives on the case did TV spots and the family got groups of people out looking for her but no leads were ever found. The case was eventually handed over to their cold case detective. He spent a lot of time trying to get answers and wasn't getting anywhere on the case so he asked a lady who had worked for their department before if she would help. This lady had an unusual gift of being able to communicate with dead people. She's so good at doing this that she's been able to help solve some of the cases in their department. I've got her name and number. Do you think she might be able to help us with the Birchim case?"

"Why not give her a try? I can't see any harm in it."

"I'll give the Denver detective a call who used her. I'm curious how she works. I also want to know just how helpful she really was."

After fielding some phone calls and shuffling papers on my desk, I decided I'd get a sandwich to eat for lunch before making my call to Denver.

"I'm going to head down to the food trucks across the street. Do you want to come along?"

"Thanks, but no thanks. I'm right in the middle of returning two phone calls and need to keep at it."

It was warm with a slight breeze as I made my way across the street to the food trucks. Three were parked along the curb and each specialized in a different cuisine. Now I had to decide between Mexican, Asian, and burgers. I decided on a bowl of rice noodles with chicken and veggies at the Asian truck instead of a sandwich. The aroma coming from the bowl smelled delicious as I crossed the street and found a spot on a park bench overlooking a small lake behind our office. It felt so peaceful, watching the mallard ducks swimming in small circles hoping for one of the picnickers to throw a crumb of bread to them. I slurped my Asian noodles and took in the sounds of nature. Birds were chirping and bees were buzzing while children played hide-and-seek around the trees. This idyllic setting washed away the frenetic pace of the office and seemed to calm my mind.

All of a sudden, an idea popped into my head like a jet breaking the sound barrier. I decided I really needed to come here for lunch more often.

My Denver phone conversation proved fruitful. I felt much more confident in this lady, who had helped the cold case department, that she was the "real deal" and not some kind of wacko. Her name was Tracy and I liked her at once as I had a cute lop-eared bunny named Tracy a few years ago.

I placed a call to Tracy, left a voicemail message introducing myself, and asked her to call me directly. This was going to be a new experience for me and I wasn't sure how I would prepare for it.

The phone call came in at the end of the work day. Tracy apologized for not calling me sooner. I told her I'd gotten her name from a detective she had worked with in Denver and hoped she could help me. Her suggestion was for us to meet in Denver at her house. She said to plan for at least two days with her and three if I could take that much time. We both looked at our calendars and decided on Thursday of the following week.

Now that the meeting was set, it was time for me to approach Daniel with my idea.

"It came to me that since Barbara Birchim, Jim's wife, has been working on this case for more years than anyone else, she might understand information coming through Tracy that we wouldn't even pick-up on. What if we asked her to come with us?"

"Sounds like a good idea to me. It certainly couldn't hurt and she might have some questions we hadn't thought of."

"I'll give her a call right now and get things rolling."

Within thirty minutes, I had confirmed with Barbara that she would go with us. She said she wanted to book the airline and hotel reservations for the three of us as she had lots of frequent flyer points that were about to expire. I accepted her gracious offer. This was going to be an interesting trip.

Guess it was time to book the sitter for Lucy.

CHAPTER THIRTY-SEVEN

The weekend zipped by as I had all the housekeeping, laundry, gardening, and grocery store things to get done before Monday.

We were to leave at the end of the workday on Wednesday which gave both of us time to plow through some of the other cases on our desks. I brought my suitcase to the office on Wednesday so I wouldn't have to make the trek back home and feel bad about leaving Lucy when I saw her. Barbara would meet us at the airport so we could all go together.

The altitude is higher in Denver than where I live and I started noticing a slight headache coming on when I stepped off the aircraft. By the time we walked, for what seemed miles to get our luggage, I was huffing and puffing to catch my breath.

The hotel was beautiful and our rooms were on the top floor with a view. The rugged, snowcapped mountains were gorgeous and such a different sight compared to our beaches and palm trees in California.

Before the three of us retired to our separate rooms, we decided we'd meet for breakfast in the downstairs café at 8:00 a.m.

I decided a nice cup of tea and a sandwich from room service were just what I needed before crawling into bed. I started thinking about all the information we had on this case and wondered if we'd ever get an answer to what really happened. There were odd parts of this story but no glue to tie them together. Were the answers buried so deep in archives that we'd never find them? Would we ever find someone who was really going to give us the whole story? In despair, I tried to connect these stories in some kind of logical fashion but kept coming-up short.

Thoughts of what to expect from tomorrow's meeting ran through my head as I slid between the crisp white sheets.

CHAPTER THIRTY-EIGHT

On the way to Tracy's house, Daniel said, "Barbara, we think you should take the lead in dealing with Tracy. If we think of any questions that aren't covered today, we can wait until tomorrow to ask them. You know much more about this case than we do."

"That sounds like a good idea. I really don't know how this is going to work, but maybe too many questions being posed at once would be a little disturbing to Tracy's concentration. What did you tell her about Jim?"

"The only thing we told Tracy was your husband's name. She didn't even ask for anything else."

Tracy lived in a middle-class neighborhood and as we parked in front of her house, we noticed the neighbor mowing the lawn and children playing hop-scotch on the sidewalk. Every yard had trees and flowers bordering the houses which made the scene look like a Thomas Kinkade picture. A lady was standing at the front door waiting to greet us. She was average height, about 58 years old, with salt-and-pepper colored hair done in a bob, and she was wearing a marine-blue dress. Her smile was welcoming as we walked into her living room. Her living room was warm and inviting with two couches done in blue-green floral prints, cream carpeting, a small fireplace, an easy chair, and tables-chairs-lamps in various places.

After introductions, Tracy told us about her background and hoped that she could help us get information on our case. She said that her "gift" had been with her since she was a young child and she remembers being surprised when she discovered not everyone had it. Her family never made her feel like this was anything unusual. They were just surprised at times when she told them who had visited with her.

Our session started by Tracy telling us she had put Birchim's name on a piece of paper and affixed it to her refrigerator. Every time she walked through the kitchen, she asked out loud if Jim would please come forward. After two days, she didn't have to ask any more as he was around the house most of the time. As we listened, she said, "He's right over there now. What I don't understand is he's wearing camouflage military clothing and there are a lot of men behind him wearing the same. Does this make sense to you?"

Barbara said, "Yes."

"He says he really doesn't want to remember what happened because it's too painful."

"I'm sorry if this is upsetting to him but the family really needs to know what happened to him."

"He says there are things you really don't want to know about this."

"Please. The family has gotten bits and pieces of information for over fifty-three years but we need validation that the information is true."

"He's nodding his head, okay. He says you know he was the leader of a ten-man team inserted into Laos when they were attacked by the enemy. For three days, they used their escape and evasion training to avoid the enemy."

Jim is saying, "I think I broke my ankle and I had shrapnel in my back but I kept my team together. Two of my men got killed and all the others suffered wounds. On the third day, I called in air strikes on top of us because we were surrounded by the enemy. I asked for extraction that night because we wouldn't make it until the next morning. That's when the team got split. Four men were able to get to a partial clearing and were airlifted out. Myself, the other American, and two South Vietnamese Regular Army men couldn't keep-up the pace. The second helicopter finally saw my flare through the triple-canopy jungle and came for us. He couldn't land so he lowered four ropes down. One of the McGuire Rigs got hung-up in the trees so now there were four of us and only three rigs."

Tracy asked Barbara. "Does any of this make sense to you?"

"Yes. The incident he related is exactly what the board report stated in sixty-eight."

Tracy got quiet and just stared across the room. It was like she was waiting for Jim to continue. After a few minutes, he did but the topic shifted.

"I know about the children. I know you've gone to Vietnam and tried to find answers. I know you've gone to Washington DC, many times and confronted government men. I know you've tried your best to help me before it was too late."

This session went on for almost three hours. Jim bounced back-and-forth, giving information about his incident and things he knew happened years afterwards. The three of us didn't ask any questions, that would come tomorrow. It was like Jim was in the room with us, only the three of us couldn't see him. We could tell Tracy was looking at him because she focused on a certain place in the room where she was seeing something.

Our time for today was up as Tracy had another appointment with a detective who was also working on a cold case. We settled on a time to meet the next day and said our good-byes.

During the taxi ride back to the hotel, we were all shaking our heads at the amount of information she had relayed to us through Jim. We decided to take a small break, meet for an early dinner, and then get together to compile the questions for the next day.

Barbara had come with lots of very specific questions she wanted validated. As we listened to her questions, Daniel and I were blown-away with the amount of information she had that we hadn't seen in any documents we'd gone through or interviews we'd done. Her questions were going down a line of thinking we hadn't even considered.

The outcome of tomorrow's meeting might turn our investigation upside-down.

CHAPTER THIRTY-NINE

The air was crisp and clear as we waited for the doorman to hail us a taxi.

The ride to Tracy's seemed to fly by and each of us was feeling excited as we wondered what information would be revealed today. We each had our notes and were reviewing them as we pulled-up to her house.

The smell of fresh coffee and lemon cake greeted us as we made our way into Tracy's living room and sat down.

Tracy brought in a tray with coffee cups, a thermos of coffee, and slices of lemon cake on paper plates. "Please help yourself," she said.

Before we got started, Tracy went to the front door. I heard a clank and then the door closed. She came back into the room and said, "I wanted to put my sign on the door that says 'session in progress' so we won't be disturbed." She smiled and asked how we liked our hotel and the meal service.

Daniel, Barbara, and I all chimed in by telling her

about our different entrees and how much we were impressed with the flavor and presentation of the food.

Tracy started by saying, "When I decided to bake the lemon cake this morning, a little lady with white hair appeared in my kitchen and began to tell me about herself. She said she's your grandmother and used to do a lot of baking and her favorite recipe was for angel food cake. My goodness, she was very chatty. She introduced your grandfather but he didn't say anything. I'm guessing he was a quiet man. Is that right?"

Barbara looked shocked. "That sounds like both of them. My grandmother used to do a lot of baking and some of her favorites were angel food cake and lemon meringue pie. She also made biscuits from scratch. My grandfather loved her baking."

Tracy was staring at something across the room before she started to speak.

"Jim is also here and he wants you to know that he's always around you. He's telling me some of the things that have happened in your house are really his doing. These are things you can't explain."

Barbara said, "I know there have been many different men who have been in and out of my house while I was either at work or out of the country. Three sets of different neighbors have witnessed this and it's been going on for at least eight years. My neighbors have even seen them through my office window going through my files. Does Jim know about this?"

"He's nodding his head, yes."

Barbara comments, "I don't understand why the government would be so concerned about what I might find about Jim being missing. Afterall, if I could find Jim's body why would they care? I'd just be doing their work for them."

"He's saying there's more to this than you know."

Daniel interrupted to ask Tracy if he could tape the session.

Tracy nodded and said, "Yes. That's fine with me. Does anyone want some more coffee before we continue?"

We all headed to the kitchen to refill our mugs and get another slice of lemon cake before returning to the living room.

Barbara continued. "I think I have some answers to what really happened to Jim but I need him to validate them. I understand this isn't easy for him but I really need to know. Did Jim get on the McGuire Rig?"

"He says, no. He is saying that one of his men hit him in the head with his rifle and left him for dead."

"Was this man one of the South Vietnamese Army men?"

Jim answers, "Yes."

"Were you taken prisoner?"

Tracy said, "Wait! He's saying something to me. He wants to know why you keep asking him questions that you already have the answers to. And, you can ask him directly as he's right over there. You don't need to ask me."

Barbara turned toward the part of the room where Tracy had been seeing Jim. All Barbara could see is a recliner chair with a table next to it holding a vase of red flowers. She started her questioning once more.

"Okay. The reason I'm asking some of these questions, Jim, is because I've had to fill-in the gaps of your story with logic and my gut feeling. I want to make sure I'm on the right path. Were you taken prisoner?"

Jim's response through Tracy was, "Yes. They hauled me away and threw me in a pit with another American but he only lived another day or two. We didn't get any food and the only thing we got to drink was water when it was thrown on us through the bamboo screen covering the pit."

Tracy said. "He's really not wanting to tell you anymore."

Later, Daniel and I spoke with each other about how grateful we were for Tracy allowing us to tape this session as we were dumb struck from the information being revealed. We couldn't have taken enough notes to keep-up with the questions and answers.

"Please Jim, I need to know what happened."

Tracy continued. "Jim is saying he was moved to a hospital by the enemy. He didn't see any other Americans there. He says he was very sick and weak, but does remember one man who was kind enough to wash his face."

Barbara asked. "Was this the V211 Hospital in Cambodia?"

"He doesn't know."

Barbara presses Jim for answers. "How long were you in the hospital? Was it a week? A month? A year?"

Tracy relays his answers. "He doesn't know. He says it seemed like a long time. He's saying they closed the hospital and moved him to another location."

It must have been feeding time for Tracy's two cats because they came into the room meowing as loud as two fire trucks going to a fire. Tracy excused herself and went to the kitchen to feed her felines. While she was gone, Barbara sat in deep contemplation while Daniel and I marveled at what we were hearing. I tried to settle my mind as it was beginning to whirl like a washing machine on the spin cycle.

Tracy came back into the room and apologized for her two noisy cats. She settled herself on her recliner chair and appeared to focus on a spot across the room.

Barbara looked at the same spot and asked Jim, "During the move, did you escape?"

"He's nodding his head, yes. He is saying he was surprised his captors weren't watching him closely. When he escaped, he followed a stream bed until he was able to get to a camp with Americans," Tracy said.

Daniel and I were mesmerized by what was happening before our eyes. We could tell that Barbara and Jim were really communicating through Tracy. Daniel and I had never witnessed anything like this before.

Then, Barbara asked what Daniel and I thought was a strange question.

"Do you now know the real reason you were sent out on that mission?"

"Yes. Weeks before I was sent into Laos, I discovered a black-market ring going on in Kontum where I was stationed involving prostitution, drugs, gold, weapons, and more. Not until I was in charge of payroll did I also discover monies were being skimmed from the payrolls of the indigenous. I couldn't turn my back on that and went to my commanding officer who, as it turned out, was part of this corrupt ring. The monies they were making was huge and going all the way back to Washington, DC. They were afraid I might leak the information to the press and that would make for a big scandal. The easiest way to eliminate me was to get me killed on a mission."

Tracy was quiet for a minute before saying, "I lost my memory due to the head wound. I didn't remember anything, not my name, my childhood, my parents, and not you. The Americans took me to Kontum. When I got there, the commander realized who I really was and was shocked because I was supposed to be dead. He decided I wouldn't be divulging anything about the black-market since I had no memory. So, he gave me a new identity."

Tracy appears to be listening to something. She says to Barbara, "Jim is asking again why you keep asking these questions when you know the answers."

Barbara asked for a break as she knew the next series of questions were going to be tough and she wanted to give all of us a chance to digest what we were hearing. We talked about the weather, how beautiful the flowers were in front of her house, and numerous other mundane things just to relax our brains for a few minutes.

We started again.

Barbara said, "I need to make sure I know the truth. Please go on with what you remember."

Tracy relayed Jim's statement. "I was in really bad shape. After getting some real medical care, and resting for several weeks in Saigon, I was given a new assignment. I was stationed in Thailand and told to watch the movement of drugs through the Golden Triangle. I don't want to talk about this."

We heard a knock at the front door and Tracy mumbled something about "can't they read" as she opened it. It was her nephew who came in, apologized for the interruption, and handed Tracy a bag of oranges. Tracy thanked him and shooed him out the door shaking her head as she reseated herself in her comfy chair.

Daniel checked the recorder to make sure it was running properly while Tracy was dealing with her nephew and I took a potty break. It was good to get up and walk a bit.

Like a good detective, Barbara had anticipated that Jim might be reluctant to admit that he had remarried and had a family. So, Daniel and I weren't surprised when she made the next statement.

"Jim, you didn't remember me so I would have expected you to have a family and make a life for yourself. I have a feeling you were living in northeast Thailand. Right?"

"Yes, I lived in a small primitive village. The houses were on stilts and near a dirty river. You were in that village one time with a Sister delivering food. I didn't know who you were, but I did see you."

Barbara said, "I remember that village. It was by the Mekong River. I felt your presence there but I couldn't see you, Jim. It was like electricity surrounding me but I knew it was you. When Sister and I drove back to the convent, I felt like I was leaving you behind. I felt like I had failed you. I remember when you came in my dreams and you were pleading with me to come to you before it was too late. When I left the village, I didn't know if you were still needing my help or if you were now safe. My heart ached."

Tracy relayed Jim's reply.

"I know how much work you've done to try to find me and the other missing men. I know you went to Vietnam several times searching for me and almost got thrown into jail because of your actions. We all know."

Our two hours were up and it was time for the three of us to leave Tracy. I had been told by other detectives that she was able to get information, which helped close cold cases. In my wildest dreams, I never thought it would be this comprehensive.

Not a word was said during the ride back to the hotel in the taxi. This was good as my head felt like it was going to explode with all the information we'd just gotten.

During dinner that evening, the three of us talked about all the information we'd gotten.

Barbara said, "I'm sure you two weren't expecting the story Jim just conveyed. I've kept a lot of that information to myself because I didn't have any hard evidence to prove it. Lots of different men have given me pieces of his story but no one has put it all together. Jim just gave me the glue, which puts the pieces together. Where is Jim now is the big question."

I could tell Barbara was relieved to find out all those

pieces of information she had collected over the years were true. The smile on her face showed me her hard work was finally paying-off. It took her 53 years to get this far. The last piece to this puzzle, which is "where is Jim now", is going to be the hardest. The amount of information we gathered from our time with Tracy exhausted me but, it also gave me hope that we could find Jim Birchim.

Daniel and I were going to be busy when we returned to our office on Monday.

CHAPTER FORTY

Lucy had been up to her old tricks while I was gone. She greeted me at the front-door and had a look on her face that said, "I'm so pleased with myself. Just wait to see what I've done this time."

At first, I noticed some pillows were now on the floor and then I noticed my table cloth was under the table. I was afraid to look in the next room.

If I didn't know better, I'd think I was living with a naughty child. The bathroom had shredded toilet paper on the floor and in the bathtub. My bedroom had a vase tipped over and my shoes in the closet had been rearranged. I'm glad I closed the upstairs office door before I went to Denver. No watching Animal Planet on the TV for her tonight.

She meowed her disapproval of my absence and then forgave me by giving me a lick on my cheek. We headed to the kitchen for food all the time talking to each other.

When I looked out the kitchen window, I could see

the garden flowers and weeds had grown while I was gone. I would need to spend some time this weekend grooming my backyard.

Dinner came out of the freezer. I had made a large pan of lasagna a few weeks ago and had frozen several portions just for an occasion like this. A bottle of red wine was in my wine rack and there was some limp lettuce for a small salad, which topped-off my dinner menu.

Lucy made her way to the stack of cat food cans in the pantry and literally licked the can she was interested in. I popped the top and put it in her bowl. Her purring sounds signified she'd made the right choice.

Tonight, it was my choice of what to watch on TV. I turned on the National Geographic channel and took my seat on the couch with my wine in hand. It wasn't long before Lucy came and curled up alongside of me. We were two happy ladies enjoying each other's company.

CHAPTER FORTY-ONE

The weekend was over and time had come to get back to business.

Several of the cold case detectives were on their vacations so the office was much quieter when I arrived at work. This meant, not as many phones were ringing and the copy machine was quiet. Also, I didn't have to fight my way to the coffee maker.

Daniel and I spent the week adding our new information on Birchim to our white boards. Since we had heard a few of these pieces of the story before, we were now confident they were real and could move them to the inside of the border on our puzzle. We still had a lot of empty space in the middle. We needed to ascertain the correctness of the other bits of information we had so they could help complete the picture.

My phone rang. The receptionist downstairs told me someone was there to talk to me about the Birchim case.

I told the receptionist I'd be right down and grabbed a tablet and pen on the way to the elevator.

Standing at the desk was a tall man, about 65-70 years old, with a great build, and thick black hair. He must have a regular work-out program as he looked like he lifted weights.

I introduced myself and he said his name was Jake. I asked if he would like to follow me to the cafeteria for a cup of coffee.

"If you don't mind, I'd rather go to the coffee stand across the street. I've got some information for you that I'd rather not say here in this building," Jake said.

"That's fine with me. After we get our coffee, we can sit on a bench in the park behind my office. It's a quiet place with a little lake. We won't be bothered there."

We got our coffee and proceeded to a spot by the lake.

"I saw your advertisement asking for information on James Birchim in a veteran magazine that I take. I knew Jim in Vietnam. He was a really nice guy and very down-to-earth. All he cared about were his men and the Hmong villagers. He'd do anything for them."

A lull in the conversation took place as Jake seemed to be collecting his thoughts. He directed his attention to the lake and the ducks swimming in circles. I remained quiet, wondering what his information could be that was so sensitive he couldn't talk in my building.

Jake continued. "There were a lot of bad things going on in Vietnam and I'm not just talking about the war. So many men were involved in it and many of them are still alive. If any of them found out I was talking to you, I'd be a dead man."

I said, "I would love to have their names but I understand your concern. Can you tell me what you know without using their names?"

Just then, a fire truck came screaming down the street and Jake almost jumped out of his skin. The loud noise seemed to impact him more than most of us in the park. I'd seen others who had been in battle react this way. So, I just waited in silence until he was ready to continue.

"There were bad things going on that many of us knew about but kept to ourselves. Some of our commanders were involved in making lots of money on the side by doing illegal things. I didn't want to get involved in it and neither did Jim. There was money being made through prostitution, drugs, gold, and weapon sales. Jim and I kept this to ourselves but when Jim found out they were skimming money from the pay to the indigenous people, he couldn't let that go. He went to his commanding officer and told him."

Jake stopped again and watched some kids skating and blowing bubbles. I could tell he was trying to decide whether or not to tell me anything else. We sat for about ten minutes just watching the boaters on the lake and enjoying the breeze before he started again.

"Jim didn't know his commanding officer was in on it."

This time, Jake stopped and it was like he didn't want to continue so I asked him, "Was this the reason that Jim was sent on that mission?"

"Yes. It was obvious to me and his other friends . . . the men involved with this money scheme . . . were afraid Jim might talk to the press about everything going on to make money. They couldn't chance it and the easiest way to get rid of the problem, namely Jim, was to send him on a mission where he'd get killed. The mission they sent him on was a sham. If you look at the time the other team in trouble called for help, you'll see Jim was inserted before that call was made. And, he was inserted miles from the team in trouble and right into a hornet's nest of bad guys. I was surprised any of his men got back alive."

Jake continued telling me things I'd heard before. When he was finished, I thanked him for coming to me and asked him to keep my contact information in case he thought of anything else.

The real truth was finally coming out.

CHAPTER FORTY-TWO

I was putting some of the pieces of information Jake had just told me into our puzzle when Daniel entered my office.

"Take a look at this," I said with excitement. "I just had coffee with a veteran who knew Jim and he gave me some of the same information we've heard from other sources. Between the people we've interviewed, the medium, and the Birchim's information, they are all relaying the same facts."

Daniel stepped back with a shocked expression on his face. He was speechless for several minutes and just shook his head.

"I really didn't want to believe this could be true. I thought we might find a villager who possibly buried Birchim's body but I never imagined his story would be like this."

Larry, the office manager, walked in and looked around. He appeared stunned with what he saw. He hadn't been in my office for several weeks and between the white boards, files, and sticky notes, he said, "I can't believe my eyes."

"I guess I should ask how your case is coming along," Larry said.

Daniel was first to reply. "We've made a lot of progress. Our informants have come forward with information confirming a lot of Jim's story. We still have a few pieces coming from only one source so we aren't sure if the information is true."

"The difference in the amount of information you gave at your first briefing and what you have now, is remarkable. Keep up the good work," Larry said as he walked out of my office.

We wanted to pat ourselves on the back for a job well done but in reality, we wouldn't have been this far with our case if our contacts hadn't been brave enough to come forward.

Daniel and I just smiled as we looked at the white boards.

CHAPTER FORTY-THREE

For the next five months, things came to a screeching halt on the Birchim case. This gave me time to dig through some of the other cases that had been on my desk for months. I was able to get resolution on several cases, but the one that was always upper most on my mind was the one on Jim Birchim.

Daniel and I had had such good luck with the incoming flow of information on that case. It looked like we were going to be able to find him. However, neither Daniel nor I had a security clearance, which meant we couldn't read classified documents. Since Birchim was a part of Special Operations, it meant all of those documents could be classified. If Birchim hadn't known about the black-market ring, I bet all of his files would be open to us. Daniel and I were stymied. We both hated waiting for something to happen.

My phone rang. A body had been found and the lead detective thought it might be one of my cases. He said the remains were being sent to the morgue and asked me to meet him there.

Good. Something to take my mind off the Birchim case.

CHAPTER FORTY-FOUR

Dick was a detective at the Police Metro Station. He and I went through police training together before we each became detectives. He always had a keen eye for details and was able to close his cases in record time. I was curious as to why he had called me in on this one.

"The body was found in a shallow grave just off the interstate by the road crew clearing brush. It looks like it's a female, maybe 20-25 years old. She was wearing those clothes on the exam table and this heart necklace," Dick said.

I looked at the clothes and necklace she'd worn. "Did you notice the initials engraved on the back of the necklace? It looks like S.L.G which could stand for Susan Lynn Grover. I'd have to review her case but I think she was in her early twenty's when she went missing. I also have a list of the clothes she was last seen in, which could help us identify these remains."

"I had a funny feeling this might be the lady you have been looking for, that's why I called you," Dick said.

I told Dick I thought there was a photo of the missing girl in my file and I'd send it to him.

"I think the family gave a DNA sample, so let's wait till we get word from the pathologist as to whether or not this is a match with your Jane Doe before we notify the family. I'd hate to get their hopes up for nothing," I said.

"I agree. The pathologist will also tell us how long he thinks the body has been in the ground. His time frame may or may not fit your case."

Dick and I spent a few minutes catching-up on what was going on in each of our lives. He had a wife and kids, and I had a cat. Enough said.

Then, it was back to the office to pull the case on Grover and call it a day.

Larry was standing at the elevator when I returned. I told him I'd been at the morgue and was hopeful we might be able to close the case on Grover.

"Good news. The family has been waiting a long time to get an answer," he said.

"I'm going to pull the case file and send Dick some information I have before I head home."

When I opened Grover's file, a picture of Susan was staring at me. She was wearing the same clothes lying on the morgue table and there was a heart necklace around her neck. Bingo!

CHAPTER FORTY-FIVE

The reports on the DNA samples came back as a match.

Closing a case is gratifying but notifying the family is tough. As long as a person is missing, there is still hope they will be found alive. Even if it isn't realistic because many years have passed, there is still hope. I knew this wasn't going to be easy for the Grover family.

I asked Daniel and Fr. Mike, our in-house clergyman/ detective, to come along with me on this notification.

When the front-door to the Grover's house opened, the expression on Mr. Grover's face changed from a smile to a look of sadness.

We were ushered into the living room while the family gathered to hear what we had to say. After introducing Daniel and Fr. Mike, I gave Mr. Grover a copy of the DNA report, a picture of the clothes the deceased was wearing when she was found, and I handed him the engraved locket. The tears started flowing as the documents and locket were passed from one to another. There was a feeling of deep sadness and relief, the long wait was over.

CHAPTER FORTY-SIX

The weeks kept going by without any information coming-in on the Birchim case. I was able to close some of the other cases I'd been working on, which was good. However, the numerous white boards kept staring me in the face with the information on Jim. Somewhere in this mess of information, there had to be the answer we were looking for.

A memo had been laid on my desk saying Larry was going to retire and plans for a party would be forthcoming. I found it hard to believe Larry had been in this office for as long as he had. Would I be able to solve the Birchim case before I retired, started running through my brain.

It had been several months since I'd talked to Barbara and maybe she had gotten more clues to Jim's whereabouts. I gave her a call and she invited me to her house. We decided the best time for me to come was after dinner so I said I'd be there at 7:30.

As I was driving home from work, I started hoping I could find some more "glue" to piece together the Birchim case.

It was time to have dinner and give Lucy a hug.

CHAPTER FORTY-SEVEN

Barbara has a dog named Scratch who met me at the door with a big "whoof." As soon as the front door was opened, Scratch was wagging his tail and was friendly as could be.

Barbara greeted me and offered a glass of white wine as we made our way to the den. I never pass up white wine.

Our conversation started with mundane chatter about the weather and politics. Then, Barbara asked me if I'd ever read about "remote viewing."

"I've just finished a book on this and found it very interesting," Barbara said. "This was a secret program our government started called Stargate. Men who were willing to submit to a psychic program were selected. They were trained to go to specific targets by using their mind."

I sat mesmerized as Barbara continued.

"It's got me thinking. If the government could do this

for an enemy target, why couldn't they do it to find our missing men?"

I was so startled by this question, I had to ask. "You mean the government isn't using this program to help find our missing men?"

"Not that I'm aware of. Some of the other books I've read deal with other kinds of programs, which may have answers for why Jim never tried to make contact with me if he ever got any of his memory back," Barbara said. "Have you ever heard of MKULTRA? That's the code name for the CIA mind control program."

Scratch came out of the kitchen, sat down in front of me, and starting scratching. Now I know how he got his name. I gave his head a pat while Barbara got the wine bottle to refill our glasses.

"If Jim started to get his memory back, it sounds like our government had ways to erase what he was beginning to remember," I said.

While Barbara replenished our glasses with wine she said, "I think that's very possible. If they wanted him to be a covert operator they never had to account for, if things went sideways, this would be the way to do it. Would you like to borrow the books on these programs?"

"I would like to borrow them. It would give me an insight into a program I didn't even know existed," I replied.

The hours were getting late, so I said good-bye and left with an arm load of books. This was going to be heavy reading.

Lucy would have to watch Animal Planet while I read.

CHAPTER FORTY-EIGHT

Thoughts of the government creating mind control programs kept running through my head as I poured my morning cup of coffee. The possibilities of them using this on anyone was scary. I'd seen two movies, "The Manchurian Candidate" and "Jason Bourne," and wondered if Birchim had been put into this kind of situation.

I waved at Daniel to come into my office. He entered, carrying a cup of hot tea, and took a seat across from me. I told him about my visit last night with Barbara, the new information she gave me, and the books I needed to read. He had heard whispers about the MKULTRA program but not about "remote viewers." We were both wondering just how deep we could dig on the Birchim case if Jim was or had been involved in this. We agreed that we needed to stay focused on a location for Birchim and put the possibilities of his involvement in one of those psychic programs to the side. Our best place to start was at the pick-up zone in Laos where only three men were extracted.

I gave Daniel a couple of Barbara's books to read. When he was finished reading those, we'd swap for the ones I'd finished. We both needed to know what we might be up against in the event we found Birchim alive.

CHAPTER FORTY-NINE

Months were flying by and Christmas was almost here. My mother planned to come for a visit during the holidays as Dad had passed away years ago and this time of the year was always difficult for her. We had a good relationship and we always enjoyed putting up the decorations. This year, I decided to splurge and get a real Christmas tree. It would be interesting to see how Lucy would react to having a live tree in the house.

When Mom arrived, the tree was standing bare-naked in the living room with boxes of ornaments spread all around. She didn't like clutter but a smile came across her face as she surveyed the scene. Peaking-out from behind one of the big boxes was Lucy. Mom put her suitcase down and immediately went over to pick her up. It was love at first sight for the both of them.

The first evening was spent catching-up on family news and Mom's plans for traveling in the near future.

She did love to travel and had been to over 50 different countries. It must have been genetic because I loved to travel, too, and was looking forward to exploring countries on my bucket-list when I retired.

CHAPTER FIFTY

It didn't seem to matter to Mom or Lucy that I had to work for the next couple of days. The two of them became best pals and continued to decorate the house while I was gone. One of the best things about having Mom visit is that she cooks dinner. I always put-on a couple of pounds when she visits me.

I took some vacation days so we could go shopping and do "girly" things before Christmas Day. This included making cookies to share with my neighbors and friends.

Daniel came by one evening with Rip, his friend's dog, to wish us a merry Christmas. Daniel hadn't met my mother and Rip hadn't met Lucy. I wasn't as worried about Daniel and my mother as I was about Rip and Lucy. What surprised all of us was Lucy and Rip got along just fine. Lucy showed Rip where the presents were and Rip didn't rip them apart. The adults had an adult beverage while the animals had a sniffing contest. All of us seemed to enjoy the evening.

I asked Daniel if he had plans for dinner on Christmas day and when he said no, I invited him to enjoy a feast with Mom and me. I knew she would go all out by making numerous dishes of yummy food that could be easily shared. Besides, what's Christmas without family and friends.

CHAPTER FIFTY-ONE

The holidays were over. Since mom had flown home, I decided to take down the Christmas tree and put away all the ornaments. The house looked dull. I'd have to get some flowers to spruce-up the living area and my bedroom. Even Lucy was moping around. I guess she missed my Mom and the tree. I think there might be a new show about animals starting tonight on television, which might make Lucy feel better.

As the office elevator doors opened, it sounded like a gaggle of geese all squawking about what happened over the holidays. I could tell what people got for Christmas when they walked in. The men all had new ties on and the ladies were wearing new blouses and jewelry.

Someone had made a tall pile of mail on my desk along with a stack of phone messages. It would take me all day and then some before I could see my ink blotter again.

One of the messages looked very intriguing. I

remembered Daniel talking about this fellow. I needed to find Daniel and hear what he knew about him.

Daniel was hard at work trying to clear his desk when I walked up. "I have a message to call Bill. Isn't he your friend on the East Coast?"

"I haven't talked to Bill in weeks. The last time we talked was about Vietnam and I mentioned the Birchim case. Do you want me to give him a jingle? Or do you want to handle it?"

I thought about the idea for a split second and said, "Why don't you call him. You've got history with him and he might be more willing to talk to you rather than me."

"You got it. I'll let you know what he says as soon as I finish talking to him."

Over all of our intercoms came the friendly voice of Larry's receptionist telling us that his retirement party was going to be tonight at Charlie's Restaurant. It would be at 6:00 and "don't be late."

I tried to take care of most of my phone messages before I left for the party but phone messages are like fungus. They seem to multiply quicker than you can get rid of them.

Charlie's was packed. Besides our department, many other floors in our building were also invited to Larry's party. The noise level was high and the drinks were flowing like water over a dam. There were going to be lots of people at work tomorrow with headaches.

Larry got oodles of kudos from his close friends. His boss made a great speech complete with jokes and then presented him with a gold watch. Some of his friends were asking him if he was going to hock the watch and buy the boat he had his eyes on. Everyone laughed but Larry was no doubt going to do just that.

My feet were killing me so I decided to call it a night and left the party about 10:00. Lucy was going to be very mad at me because I was arriving home way past her dinner time.

CHAPTER FIFTY-TWO

Days had passed before Daniel could make contact with Bill. While he was working on that, I continued to tackle my stacks of papers. If I couldn't get some of these taken care of, I'd be hidden behind them. I'm not very tall and these were closing-in on me.

The work day had almost come to an end when Daniel notified me that he'd made contact with Bill. I asked Daniel if he wanted to come over to the house for a drink and he could tell me what Bill said. When Daniel said, "Yes," I told him he could bring Rip since Rip and Lucy seemed to be friends.

Daniel and I left the office at the same time. He said he'd walk Rip over to my house and would be there in about an hour. This would be just enough time for me to see if Lucy had destroyed anything, feed her, change out of my work clothes, and get some glasses out of the cupboard.

One of Daniel's traits, which I love, is punctuality. I

can count on him from being one minute before to five minutes after the arranged time.

When Rip started barking at the front door, Lucy knew her friend had arrived. Once the door was opened, the two of them ran off to play while the adults made their way to the kitchen to get a drink.

Daniel and I did a recap on Larry's retirement party before getting into the information Bill had given Daniel.

Daniel needed to tell me about Bill before he got to the punch-line. "During the war, Bill was a medic. It was really hard on him when he got back to the states. Besides all the political stuff that was being thrown in our face when we returned, he had horrible nightmares about the men he couldn't save."

Daniel stopped and took a swig of his beer before starting again. I topped-off my wine glass.

"It took me several years before I could convince Bill to get some counseling. He was at a breaking point when he finally agreed to talk to someone. I'll fast forward and say that during his recovery he discovered something else about himself. He discovered that when he got into a deep meditation, he could visit with people he knew had died. He started with the men he couldn't save. He can now visit with anyone. Does this sound familiar?"

A smile came across my face as I picked-up a book on the coffee table about "remote viewing." I turned it around so Daniel could see it. He nodded his head "yes," while we both sat looking at each other in amazement.

The calm was suddenly broken when Lucy came flying by with Rip in hot pursuit. Bang! Daniel and I jumped up. Lucy was now stuck under a cabinet and Rip was wagging his tail. It was time to call a "time-out" for our "kids." Daniel pulled Rip away and I got Lucy out from under the cabinet. She didn't look like she was missing any fur. Being her turn to do the chasing, off they went to the bedroom. I wondered if this happened with real kids.

Daniel continued. "I think it would be a good idea if we made a trip to the East Coast to meet with Bill. He said he was willing to try contacting Birchim for us."

"You're right. We need to see if he can give us any more clues on this case. I don't think we should ask Barbara to come along this time because we don't know how credible Bill's information will be. With Tracy, we knew she had worked with the police department on solving cases and had a good track record. Besides, three people showing-up at Bill's place might put him off. Let's plan to meet with him soon."

CHAPTER FIFTY-THREE

Several weeks passed before we could arrange a meeting with Bill. During those weeks, I was able to clear a couple of cases off my desk, which meant I could now see the white boards against the wall in front of me.

Our weekly department meeting started with an introduction to Fred, our new office manager. His background included years with the police metro station and working with the counter terrorism task force. Thoughts ran through my head of the possibility he might have inroads into information we were denied. I decided to have a meeting with him and ask if he could access classified documents. Before our meeting the next day, I sent him the case file on Birchim so he could acquaint himself with the information we'd already gotten.

"Sir, Daniel and I have been having problems getting anyone to look in classified files for us."

"Stop right there. First of all, call me Fred and not Sir. There's no need to get formal in here."

"Yes, Sir. I mean Fred," I replied.

"Now to your problem of cracking into classified files. I do have a friend in the CIA who might be able to help. Can you be more specific about the kind of information you are looking for?"

"We would like to know Birchim's new arm, if possible, and his present location. If that can't be divulged, then where was Birchim's last location during the war. If your friend's location site is different than the documents we have, we could widen our search for information."

"My friend and I will be seeing each other this weekend and I'll try to get him to help," Fred said.

I said my "thank you" and then told Daniel about my meeting with the boss.

Daniel and I were leaving for Boston next Tuesday and I hoped we'd hear from Fred if his friend was willing to help us before we left.

CHAPTER FIFTY-FOUR

I love Boston clam chowder and was looking forward to gorging on it while Daniel and I were in Boston to see Bill.

As Daniel and I fastened our seatbelts for our plane flight to Boston, my cell phone went off. Fred's contact was out of the office and wouldn't be back for a week. Phooey! Guess we don't have a choice but to wait.

The weather in Boston was perfect for a Fall day. The sky was blue and temperature was a balmy 55 degrees. I'd brought my coat, which hadn't been out of the closet in years. It felt good to feel a change in seasons.

The hotel was decorated with brown and orange colors, adding the feeling of Fall to the lobby. Carved pumpkins were on the reception desk and a funny looking witch was standing in one corner when we checked-in. A message from Bill was waiting for us as we signed the register. The note said he'd be out front of the hotel tonight at 7:00 to pick us up.

Daniel and I hurried to our rooms to stow our things before meeting in the lobby for Bill's arrival. While we waited, we talked about what we hoped would be revealed during this meeting.

CHAPTER FIFTY-FIVE

Bill lived on the thirty-fourth floor of a newer looking high-rise building in the heart of Boston. It was obvious he had hired a decorator because everything looked like the pictures in Architectural Digest and Home Beautiful. He even had a butler who opened the front door when we all arrived.

We were ushered into a large room with floor to ceiling windows overlooking a spectacular view of the city. A bar with mahogany paneling surrounding it was at one end of the room with glasses already set for us. While drinks were being poured, I gazed around taking in the large bookcases on each side of the marble fireplace. A grand piano was located in one corner and couches and stuffed chairs were scattered around. It was a very masculine setting.

With drinks in hand, we all seated ourselves next to the fireplace. Bill gave us a little information on his background. He had been in Vietnam with Daniel during the war, he was single, and the CEO of a financial institution. We told him a little about ourselves and the kind of work we do.

Bill said, "When Daniel told me you were looking for information on Jim Birchim, I knew I wanted to help. Jim and I crossed paths a couple of times in Kontum but never got to know each other very well. I was there when his team came back without him and I always thought the whole story was a bit fishy. Since I know the approximate area where his team was being extracted, I've been using that as my starting point when I go into my meditative state."

Bill spent the next two hours telling us what he had "seen" during his three "visits" to the site. Daniel and I were struck by the similarities of specific points that had been made previously by Tracy. Jim had been taken prisoner, held for 1-3 years, been in a hospital, escaped his captors, was given a new identity, and continued to live in Thailand after the war. I was wondering if there was any way Bill could have contacted or had known Tracy and gotten the information from her?

Before we left Bill, I asked him if he was able to help anyone else using this new gift of his and if so, would he mind giving us their contact information. He didn't mind and the first name he mentioned was a name Daniel knew. This was all we needed. Now we could verify the accuracy of Bill's ability. I also asked him if knew Tracy. His answer was "no."

Daniel thanked Bill profusely and asked him to contact us if he got any more information on Birchim.

This had been an amazing trip and our puzzle was really filling in. One thing was certain, information was being withheld by government sources.

CHAPTER FIFTY-SIX

What was I going to do when my cat sitter graduated from high school and went off to college? If I had any more cases like the Birchim one, I might have to bring Lucy along with me when I went out of town. Maybe one of my girlfriends would take her. I should probably start asking them.

Lucy was happy to see me as I pulled my rolling suitcase into the house. She was meowing like crazy, like a mother scolding her daughter for something she'd done wrong. All it took to stop the noise was a bowl of her favorite cat food. While she ate, I turned on the sprinklers in the front and back gardens, and sorted the mail.

This evening would be about Lucy so I turned on the TV to the Animal Vet. It didn't take but a few minutes before Lucy had run off to my bedroom and was hiding under the bed. I guess she didn't like the vet. I pulled her out from under the bed and reassured her the vet couldn't come through the TV and we'd turn the channel to the Animal Planet. All was well again.

CHAPTER FIFTY-SEVEN

Daniel and I sat through the morning briefing and then started putting more pieces of our puzzle together. The information on our white boards was now becoming more consolidated and we were able to eliminate one of the boards completely. We now had the same information from three different and unrelated sources. This meant these pieces couldn't be fabricated.

Was it time for us to meet with Barbara Birchim and tell her about the information we now had? Daniel and I decided the time had come. When I called her to say we wanted to update her on what we had discovered, she invited us to a family picnic on Saturday. She said she'd like everyone to hear what we had to say on Jim's case. I told her some of the information might be disturbing. Her reply was, "Nothing would surprise us now. We've imagined every possible scenario, both good and bad. We just want to hear the truth."

Barbara gave us the time to arrive on Saturday. I told her I'd bring potato salad and Daniel would bring some wine.

CHAPTER FIFTY-EIGHT

It was a perfect day for a picnic in Barbara's garden. Her flowers were all blooming, the sky was blue, and it was a balmy 74 degrees.

When Daniel and I arrived, there were ten adults and six children milling in and out of the house and the garden. Platters of food were in the kitchen ready to be set out when meal time arrived.

Barbara told us to help ourselves to the beverages and then come outside so she could introduce us to her family. Daniel placed his bottle of wine with the other adult beverages and I put my potato salad in the refrigerator. We got our drinks and went outside to join the family members.

We were introduced to each person before Barbara asked everyone to take a seat as we had some information for them on Jim. The mood shifted from happy and gay, to quiet and somber.

I started by explaining what kind of work Daniel and I do. Then, I shared all the information we had gotten from Tracy in Denver, John in Costa Rica, and Bill in Boston. I told them we had many other veterans contact us but their information wasn't as compelling as the three

I just mentioned. I also said we were trying to get an inroad into classified documents that might also help our investigation.

There wasn't a sound as I spoke, not even from the children. I felt like the scene in front of Daniel and me had frozen in time. No one moved. The expressions on the faces in front of us were of people shocked and in disbelief. It took almost five minutes before anyone said a word.

The questions, which were asked, were the same ones we wanted answers to. What was Jim's new name and where was he? I told the family I hoped our contact in the CIA would be able to give us those answers.

A look of resolution filled their faces as they thanked us for all our hard work.

Not until one of the children started playing and chasing a dog did the mood move back to a happier one. During the picnic, family members came up to Daniel and me and asked other questions. Some we could answer like "did Jim get lifted away from the pick-up zone" and some we couldn't like "is he still alive."

As Daniel and I got ready to leave, Barbara told us how grateful she was for coming and sharing this information. She said, "I know how difficult it is to think you are finally going to get the important information you want and it turns out to be a dead-end. It's so frustrating."

On the drive home I thought about the family, their

emotions, and the heartache they've had to endure since 1968. All cold case families must go through the same kind of heartache but this was the only case I was working on that had gone on this long. I still felt a heaviness in my heart as I pulled into my driveway.

Lucy was at the window watching for me as I walked to my front door. She always lifts my spirits.

CHAPTER FIFTY-NINE

Fred took me aside after the morning briefing and told me he had made contact with his friend in the CIA. His friend had done some investigation from his end on James Birchim and had run into a wall. It looked like Birchim had been put into a secret program similar to the witness protection program. Unfortunately, even with his security clearance, he wasn't able to access it and he didn't know what arm of the government controlled it. Everything and everywhere he tried led him to "Access Denied."

Daniel and I decided we needed to go back to Army Casualty and the Defense POW/MIA Accounting Agency (DPAA) and keep pressuring them to go to Laos and search for Birchim. We really didn't know if we had any ability to move these agencies when the family had spent years trying to get them to listen and act on information on the case. Anything was worth a try at this point.

Our only other hope was for an ex-pat, living in Thailand, to come forward with information on Birchim.

We had kept in contact with our sources there and knew they continued to look for anyone resembling the photos of Jim, which we had left with them. Our feelers in the Special Ops and Special Forces communities were still out there and now it was a waiting game to see if any information would come to us.

CHAPTER SIXTY

It was Lucy's birthday so I decided to have a party for her. I invited Daniel and Rip to a backyard celebration for my dear feline friend. Special treats were made for both Lucy and Rip and placed on colorful paper plates awaiting the proverbial singing of Happy Birthday. Both Rip and Lucy sat patiently on the lawn as Daniel and I sang, clapped, and placed the treats in front of them. It wasn't until then that I noticed gray whiskers and hairs on Lucy. I guess the sunshine was hitting her fur just right and made the gray visible.

Daniel and I enjoyed the afternoon in the sun, relaxing and talking about anything except work. While partaking in adult beverages, we watched our furry friends chase each other and play hide-and-seek in my garden. When the time came for Daniel and Rip to leave, I could tell Lucy was wishing her friend could stay. I really wasn't ready for that kind of a sleep-over.

When bedtime arrived, I took a hard look in the mirror

as I brushed my teeth. I, too, had some gray hairs showing like Lucy. Yikes! I really never paid much attention to my birthday, but now I could see the years were starting to show on my face. That really hit me. How many years had I'd been working in the cold case department? And, how many years before that at the police metro station? I guess it was time to think about retirement or at least explore my options. I really didn't like thinking about this, but an exit strategy is better than being caught off-guard. I'd have to call my financial planner and get some advice.

CHAPTER SIXTY-ONE

Between meetings and answering phone calls, I managed to find the regulations on retirement. It looked like I was nearing that awful age when retiring was mandatory. This can't be happening. I had cases I'd been working on for years that I wanted resolved before I left the department. It looked like I'd have only one year to get all of this done.

The months rolled-on and some of my cases were able to be closed but the one staring me in the face each day was the one labeled Birchim. No new information was forth coming and the government kept saying they weren't able to search Birchim's site in Laos due to the country prohibiting them from entering that area.

If Birchim had died in 1968, the acidity in the soil in Laos would be eating the bones away at a rapid rate. Each day there would be less and less for the recovery team to find. If Birchim had a new identity, like our three credible sources said, he would be 75-years-old and after all he had to endure, could he live much longer? Time was running out to find him.

CHAPTER SIXTY-TWO

Eleven months had passed and I now had fewer white boards staring at me because Birchim's puzzle had filled-in dramatically. Unfortunately, the final pieces were still missing.

I could hear plans being made in the office for my retirement party. The end was drawing near.

The Birchim file was upper most on my mind. I needed to find someone in the office to take-over the case. Daniel was the obvious choice, but he had only five more years before he had to retire. I needed to have a powwow with him.

Friday evening was the perfect time to invite Daniel over for a glass of wine. He gladly accepted and arrived after dinner.

"Daniel, there's something I hope you will do for me. You've probably heard the information floating around the office about having a retirement party for me."

"Yeah, it sounds like Fred is going to pull-out all the

stops. You deserve it. You've closed more cases than any other person in our department."

I sighed and said, "You've been with me every step of the way on the Birchim case. Of all the cases I've handled, this one is the most important one to me. Maybe it's because my Dad was in WWII and told me stories about what it was like when they couldn't bring all of their dead comrades home. Some were buried in foreign cemeteries, but it still isn't the same as bringing them home. I want to ask a favor of you. Would you take-over the Birchim case when I retire? You know more about it than the others in the department and I know how dogged you are in getting at the truth."

Without a hesitation, Daniel replied, "It would be an honor to continue the fight for answers. You know how I feel about our servicemen and women. I will leave no stone unturned."

With tears in my eyes, I gave Daniel a big hug and thanked him. I felt relieved. The best man I knew was taking the case.

"If you ever need any outside help with this case, please call on me. I would very much appreciate you keeping me in the loop as to how it's progressing. Let's hope the final piece to the Birchim puzzle will come before you have to retire," I said.

The heavy mood of the conversation lingered until

Lucy came speeding through the room as if she was chasing a mouse. Daniel and I both laughed at my crazy cat while we made our way to the kitchen to refill our wine glasses.

CHAPTER SIXTY-THREE

The last day had come and I was packing a box of my stuff when Daniel came into my office.

"There's no sense in moving the white boards or the work on the Birchim case. I've asked Fred if you could have my office. I hope that's okay with you," I said.

"Are you kidding? Getting your office is a real step-up from my desk in the middle of the department. Having a quiet place to work will be a real luxury. I'm hoping for another miracle, which is Fred will take all of your other cases."

"Dream on," I kidded.

The rest of the day zipped by and at five o'clock sharp Fred announced the day was over and we should all go to the Hilton Hotel for my retirement party. Wow! Normally, we go to the lunch room for this kind of function.

Fred really outdid himself in making the arrangements. He'd planned a sit-down dinner with live music and dancing. We had our choice of steak, chicken or vegetarian meal, that came with our choice of wine. When the plates had been cleared, Fred gave a speech giving me lots of kudos for my work. He presented me with a plaque and a beautiful gold watch, which left me speechless. It took a minute for me to collect myself before I could say my "thank you" and verbalize how honored I was to have worked with such a great bunch of people. The applause went on for what seemed like an eternity before Fred spoke and said, "Let's dance."

It was very late when I finally got home and Lucy was upset with me as it was way past her dinner time.

Getting to sleep wasn't easy because I kept thinking about the forty years of service I'd given to my job, the people I'd worked with, the cases I'd handled, and the people I'd met along the way. For the most part, I'd had a very satisfying career.

CHAPTER SIXTY-FOUR

During the first few weeks of retirement, I got a lot of little household jobs done, which I'd put on hold for years.

One day, while I was in the garden doing some weeding, it dawned on me. I should call Barbara and invite her over. She needed to know Daniel was now handling her case due to my retirement. I thought about it for a minute and decided I'd invite Daniel, too.

Arrangements were made and the evening had arrived. Barbara was the first to come. We went to the kitchen, got a glass of wine, and then I introduced her to Lucy. Barbara said she'd had a cat many years ago with the same calico markings as Lucy. She was about to tell me more when the doorbell rang. Daniel and Rip had arrived. I introduced Barbara to Rip before Lucy and Rip exited to the garden to chase each other. We decided to take our seats in the garden since it was a pleasant evening to be outside. As we walked through the kitchen to get to the back patio, I grabbed Daniel's favorite beer from the frig and handed it to him.

Barbara had heard rumors I was going to retire so when I confirmed it, she wasn't surprised.

"You know," she said, "over the years of dealing with Army Casualty I've been handed-off to so many new Survivors Assistance Officers (SAO) I've lost track of their names. Each time a new one handles my case, I have to start from the beginning and bring them up to the present with all the information we've gotten over the years."

Daniel and I were shocked. Didn't they read the case file?

Barbara continued, "Part of the problem is with each government department. They don't like to share the information they have on a case. In other words, there is no file on Jim that contains all the information from all the various agencies and departments. I'm the only one who probably has the most complete file on Jim. It's very frustrating and it makes me angry when I have to be the only one who is pushing my case along. The military departments don't have detectives. They have people who take calls, answer or try to answer your questions, and file the results away."

"I want you to know Barbara, that isn't going to happen with our department," I said. "Daniel has taken

Jim's case and you know how much we both want to get the answers you deserve."

Barbara was almost in tears when she continued. "There have been times like graduations or weddings when finding Jim hasn't been upper most on my mind. But when the event passes or when something triggers a memory of Jim, I'm thrown back into a feeling of desperation and hopelessness. The feeling can be so heavy on my heart and mind, I feel like I can't even move. The odd thing is, until now, I've not been able to show feelings. This is because the families of the missing men learned this behavior early on when dealing with the government. The only reason I can think of for the feelings to come to the surface now is I'm realizing I will probably never know any more of Jim's story before I die."

After Barbara left, Daniel and I just sat in silence for almost twenty minutes.

"It's hard to imagine having to bear that kind of a burden for so many years," I said. "I don't know how I could handle it if it were me."

When Daniel and Rip left, the house was quiet. Lucy curled up beside me as I said a little prayer for Daniel to get the final answers on Captain Birchim's case.

POSTSCRIPT

by

Barbara Birchim

Have you removed your detective hat and come to a conclusion? Hopefully Deborah gave you enough clues so you could, with some confidence, see what happened to Captain James Birchim from the time of the initial incident to many years later.

In writing this sequel, I tried to step into the shoes of the detective, Deborah, and play the part of a real detective. When I stepped in as Barbara Birchim, I was telling you what I actually experienced. The bits-and-pieces of information Deborah discovered were ones, which I had gotten since the writing of my first book Is Anybody Listening? A True Story About The POW/MIAs In The Vietnam War in 2005.

You've probably realized there isn't a final ending to this story. After 53 years of working on my husbands' case, I've come to the conclusion that even though the government may know the ending, I may not.

My husband, along with so many other men, fought a war in a foreign country. My battle field was here. There were no bullets flying at me, just threats to my safety and people who wouldn't listen or take me seriously. I had no commanding officer leading the way. I only had logic, which at times can be a curse. Servicemen had tours of duty for three years. My tour has been 53 years and hasn't ended.

When I walk into a room of active duty or retired combat soldiers, I feel a kinship. I, too, have survived and continue to do battle.

I'm not asking for sympathy. This was the path I was given to walk and I do it proudly. During these years, people have repeatedly said to me, "Just move on and forget about Jim." This is impossible. There is always that nagging "what if" in the back of my mind. I imagine this is the same with all families of missing loved ones and not just military families. The door to the missing never closes. The wounds never completely heal. For me, they intensify as I get closer to my death.

Will my husband ever be brought back home? Will we ever get the final pieces of the puzzle? It seems my destiny is to continue to wait and champion the cause for truth on what happened to Captain James Birchim during the Vietnam War in 1968.

Made in the USA
Las Vegas, NV
26 March 2021